My Sister
My Momma
My Wife

A novel

[Scan Barcode w/Mobile Device for more information]

My Sister
My Momma
My Wife

Shelia E. Lipsey

NorthStar
www.BonitaAndHodgePublishing.com
Cover Designed by TyWebbin Creations
www.tywebbin.com

My Sister My Momma My Wife

ISBN-10: 0983893527
ISBN-13: 978-0-9838935-2-3

First Edition July 2012
Printed in the United States of America

10 9 8 7 6 5 4 3 2 1

This is a work of fiction. Names, characters, places and incidents either are products of the author's imagination or are used fictitiously. Any resemblance to actual events or locales or persons, living or dead, is entirely coincidental.

Library of Congress Cataloging-in-Publication Data
2012904893

Distributed by
Bonita And Hodge Publishing Group (USA) LLC
Submit Wholesale Orders to:
Bonita And Hodge Publishing
Attention Order Processing
P. O. Box 280202 - Memphis, TN 38168
(901) 417-8579

Other Titles by Shelia E. Lipsey

Beautiful Ugly Series
Beautiful Ugly
True Beauty

My Son's Wife Series
My Son's Wife (Trade and Mass)
My Son's Ex-Wife: The Aftermath
My Son's Next Wife

Sinsatiable
Into Each Life
Always Now And Forever Love Hurts

Nonfiction Titles
A Christian's Perspective –Journey Through Grief

Anthology
Bended Knees
Show A Little Love

*

[Titles also available on your favorite eReaders]

Dedication

Nathaniel and Sharney Batts-Thomas

True love stories never have endings....Unknown

Acknowledgements

To Book Clubs and Avid Readers Everywhere!
To each and every one of you
out there in literary land...
I love You for loving Me!

And of course to
My Mommy
My Sons
My Grandchildren
My Sisters
My Friends

But most of all to
You, Father God!

People were created to be loved. Things were created to be used. The reason the world is in chaos, is because things are being loved, and people are being used.

Unknown

1

"What feeling is so nice as a child's hand in yours? So small, so soft and warm, like a kitten huddling in the shelter of your clasp." Unknown

Twenty-three hours, forty-five minutes, seventeen seconds. Hard, horrendous, harrowing, and horrific were some of the adjectives that described the worse pain First Lady Detria Graham had ever experienced in her life. It was almost impossible to put into words.

Stiles could barely contain his composure when Detria asked his thoughts about naming their child after his deceased mother, First Lady Audrey Graham. He shed tears like a baby smacked on the fanny after coming out of his momma's womb. And Pastor. Well, Pastor was just as big of a baby as his son. He too loved the idea that his first grandchild would be named after his precious, sweet Audrey, and he never hesitated to remind his daughter-in-law how grateful he was for her gesture.

Detria stared at her baby girl as she lay sleeping in her crib. Unfortunately, her elation over being a mother and wife quickly started to fade within weeks of giving birth. Audrey would be nine months in a few days. Time seemed to escape faster than Detria had time to blink.

Detria stretched and yawned. She still hadn't gotten quite used to all of the time it took to raise an infant. By her sister, Brooke having two boys of her own, Detria often turned to her for questions she had about parenting. Being a mother was unlike anything she had ever experienced. She took another look at her sleeping baby before she turned and walked into her and Stiles's bedroom. She sauntered over to the chaise sofa and eased her thin frame into its curves.

During her pregnancy, she had gained close to fifty pounds, but without trying to, and in less than three months, she had gone back down to her regular size eight in clothes. No one would ever be able to talk about her behind her back. If the weight hadn't come off effortlessly, Detria was geared up and ready to work her butt off to regain her curves. She had never stopped working out during her entire pregnancy. And she still did the same thing since giving birth. Five days a week she packed Baby Audrey's diaper bag, and off they went to the Y. She left Audrey in the on-site, childcare center while she attended her daily round of exercise classes.

The clock on the table showed a few minutes after seven p.m., still at least a couple of hours or more before Stiles would be home. With Stiles being either at Holy Rock or teaching his evening Religion class at the University of Memphis, Detria and Baby Audrey were alone most of the time. She tried to be as understanding as possible about his long hours. But there were nights like this when she felt lonely, somewhat depressed and maybe even a little agitated with Stiles. After all, Baby Audrey was growing fast, and Stiles didn't always seem to understand that he was missing out on some key moments in his daughter's life.

Detria was the one who had seen her crawl for the first time. She was the one who was around her day in and day out. She and Stiles had agreed that she would stay home from her job as a nutritionist for at least the first year of Baby Audrey's life. Both of them managed money well, so finances were the least of their worries. The church took good care of them, and she still received a portion of her salary, and would keep getting it for an additional six weeks.

Detria laid her head back against the cushiony soft back of the chaise lounge. She tried to relax while Audrey slept. Lord knows that she wouldn't get any help from Stiles when he came home. He would be too tired, as he often reminded her.

Detria looked at the caller ID when the phone rang. It was Pastor.

"Hello, Pastor. How are you tonight?"

"Blessed, baby, blessed. I was calling to check on my little one and you too, of course."

Detria's tight lips relaxed into a half smile. "You don't have to try to make me feel better. I know your granddaughter is the only girl on your mind. But you don't have to worry, I'm not jealous."

Detria's words were soft and kind. She understood how much Pastor adored his only grandchild. She had lost her and Stiles' first baby, all because of him, something she wrestled with still from time to time.

However, she had come to understand that she had no right to physically abuse him. He couldn't help that he had a stroke. She really had no right to blame him for her miscarriage either, but she couldn't help it.

"What is my precious one doing?" asked Pastor. His question jarred Detria from thoughts of the past.

"I just put her down not too long ago. She should sleep most of the night. At least I hope so. Most babies start sleeping all night at around four months. That's what Brooke told me, but I guess Baby Audrey didn't get the message."

"She's her own person, already," Pastor laughed. "I'm glad she's good though. Is there anything she needs?"

"No. You've already managed to spoil her rotten. I don't know what you're going to do when she starts walking and talking."

"I'm going to give her the moon if I can. I'm just thankful that the Lord has seen fit to let me live to see my first grandchild. I tell you, it's a blessing. A real blessing," he repeated. "I take it Stiles hasn't made it home yet," he said slightly changing the subject.

"You're right; he isn't here. Monday, Tuesday, Wednesday and Thursdays like clockwork." Detria sighed before she realized it. "If it's not noon day service, it's mid-week Bible study. If he isn't holding Bible study, he's at the university. If not there, he's counseling someone or visiting the sick. Sheez, it never seems to end. And it's rare for him to release his class before ten. He holds those students until the very last second."

"That's Stiles for you, but are you all right? You sound a little down."

"No, I'm fine," she lied. "Just a little tired. You know this granddaughter of yours demands a lot of time and attention."

"I'm sure she does. I wish that son of mine was around more than he is. Does he even come home during the day? There is no way he has to stay at church every day, all day long. And you told me that he seldom comes home before going to the university."

"No, he doesn't bother to come home, well maybe ever once in a blue moon, but then again that's Stiles for you. One thing I can say about my husband is that he is definitely committed to his calling. I know I shouldn't complain, even though sometimes I want to. He's doing God's work. I knew before I married him that I wouldn't be first in his life."

"Well, I'm going to have a talk–"

"No, don't do that, Pastor," Detria interrupted. "I'm fine. Everything is fine. Stiles is doing what he needs to do to take care of his family, and that family includes the sheep he leads at Holy Rock. Who am I to complain? It's not like I have to get up and go to work every morning. It'll be at least a year before I return to work. And I've decided that I'm going to assume a more visible role in the church anyway. I am the first lady, you know." Detria said almost flauntingly.

"Yes, you are indeed. You remind me of my dear, sweet Audrey. I still miss that woman. It's been almost three years since she went to be with the Lord." Pastor sighed. "Well, maybe by the time you do go back to work, Holy Rock's daycare center and academy will be in full swing."

"See, that's what I'm talking about, Pastor. Stiles has so much on his plate. This new project to open a daycare and Christian academy takes a lot of planning and time. Not to mention the entire revamping of the Children's Ministry."

Detria felt like she was forcing her words. If she voiced what she really wanted to say, she would be telling Pastor that she was fed up with Stiles being away from home all the time, tending to his church family, teaching at the university, and going about his life like absolutely nothing had changed. Her life, on the other hand, had been turned upside down. She had really enjoyed her job as a nutritionist, and she missed the people she worked with on a daily basis, but she had agreed to stay home with Baby Audrey.

Since being on leave, her client base had been assigned to another nutritionist, and she rarely heard from anyone at her job. Her life was all about Baby Audrey and her needs now, and at times Detria felt mounting resentment. She loved her little girl, but she also missed life as she'd known it before she became a mother and a wife.

Detria cocked her head to the side when she heard the sound of the door opening downstairs. "Pastor, Stiles is here. I just heard the kitchen door opening. I guess we talked him up; he's home early."

Pastor chuckled lightly. "Okay, baby. I'll let you go. Go tend to your husband, and kiss the little one for me. Goodnight."

"Goodnight, Pastor." Detria pushed the End button on the phone and dashed down the stairs.

"Hi," Stiles said as he met her just before she made the last step. He held his briefcase in his hand, and his suit jacket rested over the bend of his arm. He leaned forward and brushed her lips. "Baby, I'm so tired. It's been a long, long day." He sighed and passed his briefcase to her like she was his maid instead of his wife.

Detria took hold of the briefcase, pursed her lips for a second in an attempt to hold off on losing her temper. He stood at the edge of the steps and without asking how her day had been, or about his daughter, he started loosening his tie and walking up the stairs. “I’m famished,” he said while slowly climbing each step. He looked back at Detria who stood right behind him. “Any dinner?”

“Don’t I always have dinner ready for you?” It was getting harder not to go clean off on him.

“Whoa, what’s with the raised voice? I just asked about something to eat.”

“I did not raise my voice,” she answered and remained stationed on the step behind him. “Like always, your plate is in the microwave.”

“I’m going to take a shower and then if you don’t mind, would you warm it up and bring it to the study? Believe it or not, my day still hasn’t ended.” Stiles didn’t wait on a response. He took the last steps two at a time and disappeared into Baby Audrey’s room. Detria followed.

She watched from the doorway. Stiles leaned over the crib and kissed his daughter gently on the forehead and then turned around and exited the room without saying anything else to Detria.

Detria planted herself in front of him, his briefcase still in her hand. “I was wondering if you were going to remember that you had a daughter.”

“What is that supposed to mean?” His brows gathered and he looked at Detria with a scowl on his face as he whizzed by her.

"I mean, you come waltzing in here and the only thing you can think about is whether I have your dinner ready or not? It's not like I've been sitting here all day twiddling my thumbs, you know. I do have to take care of our daughter, and that is not easy."

"So now you're complaining? Is that what you're doing, Detria? You're the one who agreed to do the full-time mommy thing. You could have easily gone back to work after you had Audrey, but you said it would be a good idea to spend at least the first year with your daughter, which was fine with me." Stiles' temples began to throb.

Detria watched each beat of his temple. She knew he was ticked off, but so was she. She was the one who had the right to go off, not him.

Stiles looked down at her short stature, his arms wrapped inside the other. "Listen, all this lip you give me just about every time I step through the door has got to stop. I can't get a good word out of you. I hardly have a chance to set foot inside before you meet me with attitude."

"I am not about to argue with you tonight, Stiles. I'm exhausted too. You are not going to make light of me being a stay at home mom as some kind of, kind of," Detria repeated and raised her arms out toward him. Up the hall and down the stairs she went. She'd had enough of his insensitivity.

She pushed Auto Button 7 on the microwave as soon as she stormed into the kitchen. She could hear Stiles's shuffling upstairs. On the verge of tears, she stood in front of the microwave and thought about how difficult the last few months had been.

Stiles was like prince charming when he found out she was pregnant again. The miscarriage she'd had before Audrey was conceived had almost been the catalyst that broke their marriage apart. She hated to think about the drastic effect it had taken on her. She'd taken her anger and frustration out on Pastor by physically abusing him. What kind of person was she back then? If it had not been for Pastor forgiving her, and talking to Stiles, then she probably would have been his second ex-wife. *Lord, I hope that part of me never comes out again.*

The microwave beeped and brought her back to the present. She opened the door and removed the plate of green vegetables, Italian sausage and red beans and rice.

After she retrieved silverware and paper towels, Detria went into the family room and got the TV tray, and went back to the kitchen and put Stiles' plate of food and a glass of homemade Arnold Palmer tea on it. Before she could head toward the stairs, she heard Audrey crying. "Why is she awake? Lord, I hope Stiles didn't go back in there and wake her up. I do not need this tonight."

She hurried as fast as she could up the stairs with the tray of food and drink. "I'm coming, sweetheart," she said out loud to Audrey.

"Did you say something?" Stiles asked from their bedroom. The sound of his voice let her know he was still in the bathroom.

"Audrey is crying," she yelled so he could hear her.

"You got her?" he asked.

"Uggh," she said and did not answer him. She took the tray of food and drink to his study and rushed to see about Audrey.

"What is it, sweetie," she said as she picked her up and cradled her in her arms. She took two fingers and felt around inside her pamper to see if she needed changing, but she was dry. “Audrey, it’s not time to eat. It’s time to sleep. Sleep for the night.” She walked around the nursery and then went to the rocking recliner in the corner of the room and sat down. “You want your pacifier? Huh? Is that what mommy’s baby girl wants?” Detria stood back up and went over to Audrey’s crib. She didn’t see the pacifier, so she began to feel around the sides of the bed. She found it wedged in between the crib and the mattress. “Here you go.”

Audrey latched on to the pacifier like a pit bull.

Stiles came in with his bath towel wrapped around the lower half of his well-defined body. “She all right?” He walked over to his daughter and reached for her. Detria gladly passed her to him.

“She couldn’t find her pacifier. She’s fine now.”

“Hi, daddy’s girl. Hi, my sweetpea.” Stiles talked to his daughter and cuddled her in his arms. Detria, with folded arms couldn’t help smiling. Watching him with Audrey, reminded her of the Stiles she’d fallen in love with. That Stiles was kind, sensitive, loving and compassionate. Audrey cooed and grinned until her pacifier fell from her mouth, but this time she didn’t seem to miss it at all. It was like she was in baby heaven because she was in her daddy’s arm. “You’re daddy’s girl, aren’t you? Aren’t you, pretty girl?” He kissed her chubby cheeks and made funny faces at her before he walked back to Detria. “Daddy’s got to work and eat now. Be a big girl for mommy, okay?” he said in a gentle, loving tone. “I’m going to finish putting on my pajamas. Did you bring my food up?”

Detria rolled her eyes. “Yes.”

Stiles turned and walked out of the room, leaving Detria and Audrey alone - again. “Is this what *married with children* is supposed to be like? Daddy's busy, busy, busy all the time, isn't he," she whispered to Audrey. "It's hard enough dealing with being a preacher's wife and first lady." Baby Audrey nestled close to her momma's bosom. "Now I have to learn how to be a single mother even though I have a husband."

She rocked Audrey until she saw her eye lids close. She stood up and carried Audrey back to her crib. "At least someone in the Graham household seems to be relatively content," she said and covered Audrey in her favorite lemon-yellow baby blanket before she retreated to her bedroom.

2

"Complaining is good for you as long as you're not complaining to the person you're complaining about." Lynn Johnston

Stiles burped after he took the last swallow of his beverage. He got up from his office chair, picked up his plate and empty glass and went downstairs. The house was quiet. He looked at the clock in the kitchen. Twelve-thirty a.m. Detria was asleep and so was Baby Audrey. Maybe he could get some shuteye.

He didn't know what was going on with Detria lately. Practically, ever since she had Audrey, she had been acting like a totally different person, someone he didn't know. He couldn't figure it out, and he told himself he did not have the time to play into Detria's numerous temper tantrums. She was definitely becoming someone he did not like.

He washed his plate and glass and placed them inside the dishwasher. That was something else he didn't quite understand. Why wash the dishes only to turn around and put them in the dishwasher just to wash them again? But that was the way Detria chose to do things. The house was her turf, so he tried to abide by her rules.

When Detria first posed the idea of being a stay at home mom, Stiles thought it was a great idea. He would be able to enjoy his wife and daughter more often. But things hadn't been exactly the way he expected. It started soon after she came home from the hospital. Initially Stiles blamed Detria's short fuse on postpartum depression, but Audrey was going on ten months, and Detria's attitude hadn't gotten any better. If he thought about it long enough, he had to admit that she was never the same after she lost their first child. He managed to forgive her for physically abusing Pastor, something that took quite a bit of prayer and meditation. If it wasn't for Pastor, Stiles wasn't quite sure if he would have remained married to Detria or not. To know that his own wife was going behind his back and beating his sick father, was almost worse than being betrayed by his ex-wife, Rena.

Rena may have had a sexual relationship with his sister, Francesca, but at least it was before he took her to be his wife. If only she had told him the truth before he married her, maybe things would have been different. He loved Rena like no other woman, but her deceit and the fact that she also had an STD and didn't tell him that either, made it impossible to stay married to her. Yet, when he compared her to Detria he admitted only to himself that he would always love Rena.

He loved Detria too, and he certainly didn't want to be in the pulpit preaching if he couldn't keep his own house in order. He entered the bedroom and saw her turned on her side.

He went inside the master bathroom, brushed his teeth and then got on his knees and began to pray next to the fancy bathtub. When he finished he went to the bed and climbed in on his side. Detria didn't move. He didn't want to admit it, but he was glad she was asleep. He didn't want to go through explaining to her why he wasn't in the mood to have sex. It was a question he couldn't answer even if he wanted to. For some reason, over the past five or six months, their sex life had dwindled to almost nothing. What bothered Stiles the most about their lack of intimacy was that he really wasn't the least bit bothered by it.

Just as he was about to turn over from his back to his side, Detria turned over and faced him. "I'm sorry," she said. "Please don't be mad."

"I'm not mad, Detria. Now go back to sleep." He propped himself up on his elbow and leaned in and kissed her softly on the lips. "Good night."

Detria placed her arm over his waist and eased in next to him. She started kissing him on his arm. Stiles lay back down on his back.

"Honey, it's late. You need to sleep while the baby's sleeping. You know she still doesn't sleep through the night."

"Um hmm, need you remind me?" Detria answered, turning up her lips. She continued to kiss him, moving her hands up and down the length of his tall, muscular body, totally ignoring what he'd said. She planted light patches of kisses on his chest. Easing herself up, she lifted her short, satin gown and began to climb on top of him.

"Detria, I said not tonight. It's been a long day."

"I know it has. I want to give you something to help you relax," she whispered into his ear. Her kisses became more passionate and she found his lips and parted them with her tongue. He listened to her moans.

He immediately pushed her off of him with unintended force. Detria stared at him with a look of disbelief. "I'm sorry. I didn't mean to push you away like that."

Immediately, tears formed in her eyes. "Am I that much of a turn off? When was the last time we made love, Stiles?"

"Look, I don't want to have this conversation right now, Detria. I'm tired. And look, stop being so paranoid, will you. There's nothing wrong with you. It's me. What part of it's late, and I'm tired don't you understand. I want to get some sleep." He tried to kiss her on the cheek, but Detria quickly turned away.

Stiles reached over toward her. In an effort to try to make things right between them, he would show her a little affection. Pastor always told him never to let the sun go down without having solved whatever issues needed solving for the day between him and his wife. But he'd failed at doing that more times than he cared to count. "Honey, please. I said I was sorry."

Detria didn't say a word.

"Detria, let's not do this. You know we promised never to go to bed angry," he reminded her.

"I'm not angry. You said you were tired, so go to sleep."

"I love you," he told her.

"Goodnight, Stiles." Detria pulled the bedcover up higher until it covered her shoulders.

Stiles propped one arm behind his head. He didn't understand exactly why, but he began to think about Rena. The last time they talked, she told him that she was going to marry Robert.

Stiles had met Robert when Rena bought him to Audrey's funeral. In Stiles's opinion, Robert seemed like a pretty cool dude, and he hoped Robert could make Rena happy.

Robert was a much better man than he was, Stiles had concluded, because Robert accepted Rena after learning about her former lesbian lifestyle and the fact that she had contracted herpes from his sister. If only Rena had been as open with him as she was with Robert, maybe their marriage would have stood a chance. But she chose to keep her past a secret, and that was more than he could take. She had hurt him like no one had hurt him before. Never again would he allow himself to fall victim to the kind of heartbreak he endured with Rena.

Stiles closed his eyes and tried to answer the call of sleep, but flashes of Rena's smile kept replaying in his mind. *Father God, forgive me. Help me be a better husband. I shouldn't be lying here thinking about my ex or any woman other than my wife.*

He turned over on his side toward Detria. He reached underneath the cover and his hand began to explore her curves. Stiles cautiously eased her gown up and felt the warmth of her naked flesh; he became aroused.

"Go to sleep, Stiles," Detria said in a stern voice.

"Baby," he whispered. "I'm sorry." He nibbled on her ear lobe. "You know that I love you." He continued caressing her body, touching her in all the places he'd come to know she loved. He eased up close to her until his body touched hers in a spooning position. Detria moved slightly, but Stiles heard her soft moan. There was no stopping him now. He caressed the nape of her neck, her back and her arms with his mouth and tongue. Gently and slowly, he turned her over toward him. Detria didn't resist. He eased out of his pajamas bottoms. With tenderness, he lifted her gown over her head while he continued to kiss and caress her.

As he made love to his wife, he tried to keep Rena from making love to his mind. It was Detria he loved; Detria he was married to; and Detria who had given him his first child. With each thrust, he saw her rising to meet him. *Rena, Rena.*

◊

Stiles awoke in the early dawn. The house was quiet. Detria was curled in a semi fetal position. He watched the rise and fall of her breasts for a split second before a deep wave of guilt attacked him for the thoughts he'd had hours before. *Man,* wh*at's happening to me?*

Baby Audrey started crying. He looked over at Detria. Her head popped up seconds later. She looked around the bed for her nightgown. Stiles pulled it from underneath his body.

"Looking for this?" he said and half-smiled.

Detria reached for the gown. "Yea, thanks." She sat on the side of the bed and slipped the gown over her head. She moved quickly and disappeared seconds later in the direction of the nursery.

Stiles proceeded to get up and started grooming himself in preparation for another long day that would be filled with the endless responsibilities that was expected of a full time pastor. By the time he finished his morning ritual, he came out of the bathroom in his boxers and an A-shirt. Baby Audrey was sitting on the bed playing with her favorite glo-worm doll while Detria was inside the walk-in closet going through the rows of clothes on Stiles' side of the closet.

"Hi, precious. How's daddy's girl this morning?" He walked over to the bed, and picked Audrey up. Scooping her up in the air, she giggled and a long drool of slob landed on Stiles's nose. He chuckled and kept frolicking with his daughter.

Detria stepped out of the closet moments later with a black suit, white shirt and a pair of Stiles' dress shoes in her hands. She closed the closet door and proceeded to hang the outfit on the back of the door and set his shoes in front of the bed.

Stiles reached for her and held her and Audrey in the cradle of his arms.

"Stiles, stop it," Detria told him, but not in her *I mean it* voice'. He kissed her and then he kissed Baby Audrey. The more Detria tried to twist herself out of his grasp the tighter he held on to her.

"My two favorite girls in the entire world. How blessed can one man be?" he said and gave each of them another kiss. He released Detria and she immediately straightened up. When he sat Baby Audrey back down on the bed, she went straight for her baby doll again. "How are you doing this morning, First Lady Graham?" he asked with a smile.

Her response was dry. "Fine."

"You still angry with me?"

"No, I told you last night that I wasn't mad at you, so please, let's not ruin the morning with bringing up last night. Will you watch your daughter while I wash up. Then I can get breakfast started."

"Sure. What daddy wouldn't want to watch this sweet little angel," he said and laid flat on his tummy in front of Audrey. Audrey pulled on his low cut hair and slobbered on his face. Her way of kissing. He adored her. "Every day she looks more like my mother. Don't you think?"

"Umm, a little, but I like to think she looks like me." A tiny hint of a smile finally appeared on Detria's face.

"Of course, she looks like you too, but I still see my mother every time I look at her."

"Let me get washed up. I'll be out in a minute." Detria disappeared into the bathroom. Stiles heard the shower come on. He continued playing with Audrey for a few minutes before he got up and started putting on the clothes Detria had laid out for him. It was something she did every morning. She had a great taste in style, and often bought many of the clothes he wore. That part reminded him of his mother too. First Lady Audrey used to love fashion. She used to outfit Pastor like Detria was doing for him. Stiles smiled as he finished tying his tie.

Detria came out of the bathroom in her robe. She went to the dresser drawer and pulled out a pair of house pants and a matching shirt. After picking up Baby Audrey, she slipped her feet inside a pair of slides. "Breakfast will be ready shortly," she said. Without waiting on a response, Detria started to walk out of the bedroom.

"Okay, give me about thirty minutes, and I'll be down."

"Sure," she answered before she disappeared and headed downstairs. Stiles retreated to his office, like he did every morning, for his alone time with God.

◊

"Breakfast was good," he complimented his wife. "Nothing like a bowl of hot grits, and wheat toast.

"DaDa," Baby Audrey said and then blew out a mouthful of grits all over her high chair and the floor.

"Did you hear that?" Stiles wiped his mouth and jumped up. "She said Dada," he said. "She's always saying MaMa, but this is the first time I've heard her say Dada. You are such a smart little girl, Daddy's smart, beautiful little girl." Stiles took a paper towel and wiped her molly mouth.

Detria looked at him, like she wanted to tell him that his precious Baby Audrey had been saying DaDa for at least a month.

"Honey, she said DaDa," he repeated. His voice was full of excitement and awe.

Detria removed the breakfast dishes from the table and highchair. "Actually, this isn't her first time saying it."

"It's my first time hearing her, and you've never told me that she's been calling my name."

"Maybe it's because you didn't bother to ask. If you were around here–" Detria turned on the kitchen faucet. "Never mind."

"No, go on. Say what's on your mind."

"I said never...mind."

"Look, what's wrong with you now? I thought we patched things up last night. Now this morning, you still tripping."

"Why would you think that, Stiles? Because you got some? Well, you wouldn't have gotten it if I didn't let you get it. Remember that." Detria pounced around, went to Baby Audrey's high chair, and started cleaning it off. Baby Audrey continued to talk baby talk.

"I'm out." Stiles kissed his daughter. "I love you, sweetpea," he said to her before he left the kitchen, slamming the door leading to the garage behind him.

He heard Baby Audrey crying. As bad as he wanted to turn around and go back inside and comfort her, he didn't. "No drama; not today anyway," he said and climbed inside his Audi A6.

3

"One man's folly is another man's wife." Helen Rowland

Rena had exactly three days to go before her impending nuptials to Robert Becton. She walked through the bridal store with her mother, searching for last minute bridal accessories.

"Mom, what do you think about these?" Rena held up a flower girl faux pearl necklace and ring set. The ring had a lone faux pearl trimmed in sterling silver.

Meryl replied, "That is too cute. It would be perfect for Robert's little girl. You haven't bought anything to go with her flower girl dress have you?"

"No, ma'am. And I agree with you; this is so cute. I'm going to get it. She's going to love it. She is so dainty and feminine, and she's only seven years old." Rena giggled as she continued to admire the ring and necklace.

"She is that. She knows she loves to dress up." Meryl smiled.

"Okay, now let's see what we can find for the bridesmaids."

Meryl quickly corrected her daughter. "You mean bridesmaid as in one bridesmaid, and the Maid of Honor."

"See, you know what I meant." The closer it came to her second wedding day, the more Rena flip-flopped over the decision she'd made. *This is going to affect me for the rest of my life. Am I ready for this? Can I be a good stepmother to little Isabelle and Robbie, and a good wife to Robert? I don't want to fail again.*

"You know your sister won't be here until the day before the wedding. Let's make sure they've ordered her bouquet. We want everything to be perfect."

Rena snapped out of her daydream. "Sure." That's a good idea. Then all we'll have left to do is get their gifts. But, remember, Mom; this is a small, intimate wedding. Just Robert's kids and his sister plus his best man, of course. And me, well Delores is flying in from D. C. and there's you and dad."

"Honey, please, this is no time to be cheap. You're getting married; it doesn't matter the size of the wedding; it's still a wedding. Now, don't forget you said you wanted to get some type of jewelry for your bridal party." Meryl's tone of voice made it apparent that she took this wedding seriously.

"I know, Mom." Rena sighed. "I remember."

Mother and daughter spent at least two more hours shopping inside the bridal store. They left out of the store with Isabelle's flower girl jewelry set, matching pearl and rhinestone necklace and earrings sets for the bridesmaid and maid of honor, plus a dainty tiara for herself that she couldn't resist.

Rena was quite confused. One minute – ecstatic. Next minute – uncertain. One thing for sure, she believed that Robert loved her for real. He proved it by accepting her despite her past relationships with Stiles and Frankie. Rena often thought about the circumstances being switched. Would she be forgiving toward Robert like he was toward her? She didn't think that she would, or could. No, she would have reacted just as bad, or worse, than Stiles did when he found out the truth.

Robert deserved to be loved by her. Rena shook off the confusion and told herself she was ready to say "I do."

◇

"Rena, everything is fine. Your tests came back negative again. As for the herpes, you haven't had any outbreaks since you left Memphis, which has been what, three years now?"

Rena nodded.

That's outstanding news," the doctor said. "Herpes can lay dormant for years. Some people only have one outbreak their entire lives. Let's hope you're one of those. But, listen, this doesn't mean you can't pass on the virus, so still be careful." She extended her hand out to Rena.

"Thank you, doctor. This is the best news since my last visit. And you don't have to worry, I'm not taking this lightly just because I haven't had an outbreak. But it sure does feel good." Rena laughed and hugged her doctor.

"I'll see you in one year. No more every six months visits. If you have a problem or think you might be experiencing an outbreak, then of course make sure you call my office and make an appointment right away."

"I sure will. But I won't have to." Rena's confidence level was at an all-time high.

It felt good to feel free; free from her past mistakes and heartaches. Free from Stiles and his conditional love. Free from Frankie and her selfish love. Free from Pastor and his I don't have time for love, then the best one of all: free of...of First Lady Audrey and her... sick love.

When Rena arrived home she couldn't wait to tell Robert the good news.

Robert met her with a luscious kiss just as she walked inside the front door. "How was your doctor's appointment?"

"Another clean bill of health," she replied. "And I don't have to go back for one year." She raised one finger in the air and wiggled it around.

"Wow, that is great news," Robert said, laughing.

The kids ran and greeted her with squeals of joy. Seeing how much they'd come to love and accept her made her heart leap with happiness. "Hi, you guys. How was your day today?"

"My day was real, real good," Isabelle said while she bounced up and down like she'd had a little too much sugar.

"I didn't have a good day," Robbie said and jumped in front of his sister.

Rena leaned down eye level to the three year old. 'Why didn't you have a good day, Robbie?" She rubbed his full head of curly black hair.

"My teacher wouldn't let me color."

"Robbie, remember Daddy and I told you that you won't be coloring at school every day. You have to learn lots of other fun things to do. You can always color right here at home. You have lots of coloring books. Okay?"

Robbie still looked sad. "What about while I'm cooking dinner, you come in the kitchen with me and color."

His eyes opened wide and a big grin came over his face. "Yayyy."

"Okay, I'll call you when I get dinner started. Now, let me go and get out of these clothes, and you go look through your coloring books and choose one."

"Yes, ma'am," he said and ran off in the direction of his room.

"Isabelle," Rena focused her attention on her stepdaughter, "will you help me with the macaroni and cheese?" Isabelle loved being Rena's little helper.

"Yes, ma'am," she said loudly and proudly before she took off.

"And what do I get to do?" asked Robert.

"Oh, don't worry. I have something special I'd like you to do after dinner, when the kids are tucked in for the night." She gave him a sensual smile and winked. Robert reciprocated with a sly grin of his own and closed the gap between them. His lips were warm and soft. He was such a great kisser and a skilled lover too. He had a way of making her feel like she was a queen.

"Ummm," he said. "I can't..." he kissed her again. "Wait."

"Neither can I. Ohhh, guess what else my doctor told me?"

"What?"

"She said she sees no reason why we can't have a baby. Of course, she said sometimes an outbreak can occur when a woman gets pregnant, and I would have to be closely monitored if that does happen."

"I think we should follow the doctor's advice. Let's start working on that right away," His voice was hoarse as he spoke. He gently pushed her against the wall and immediately his hands and mouth were all over her.

"You are so bad," she told him and grinned. "Let me get myself together please. I have to fix dinner you know. We can't allow our children to go hungry now, can we?" She smiled.

Robert stepped back. "You're right." He raised one finger in the air. "But, you are not getting out of practice tonight, tomorrow night, the next night, or the next."

"Boy, you are crazy. I guess that's why I love you so much."

"Me love you too," he said in a boyish voice.

4

"It is so easy to be confrontive without being informative; indignant without being intelligent; impulsive without being insightful." Neal A. Maxwell

Detria opened the back door of her Prius Five and proceeded to get Baby Audrey out of her car seat. It wasn't quite eleven a.m., but Detria had already spent a couple of hours working out at the Y, on top of going to the grocery store and back home to shower and change. Now she was parked in her reserved parking space, at none other than Holy Rock.

The church membership continued to flourish. They were practically bursting at the seams, which is why they were making some extensive renovations to the church property.

Detria was glad to see the membership growth, but she still despised the extra time it took Stiles away from her. It was the main reason she decided to take on a more active role in the church by spending more time at Holy Rock. It was time Stiles and the selfish members of Holy Rock understand that she was more than just the First Lady, and the mother of their pastor's child, she was the Lady of the House.

She gathered a cooing Baby Audrey in her arms, closed the car door, and headed in the direction of the pastor's entrance to the newly expanded church building. Baby Audrey pulled on her pacifier and contently clung to her mother's dress.

Stiles had everything established for the Children's Center and the academy. What he hadn't planned on was Detria appointing herself as the administrator. But he didn't raise much of a fuss about it. He figured she would dabble around Holy Rock for a couple of weeks and that would be that. So far, it seemed that instead of growing bored with the inner workings of the church, she was growing more excited. Thus the reason she told Stiles she wanted an office at the church designated just for her.

Detria's wore a mint green, fit-and-flare knit dress that had a scoop neck, cap sleeves and a comfy pleated flare skirt perfectly accessorized with a thin buckle belt. Like her deceased mother-in-law, Detria made a fashion statement wherever she went. Without so much as a stumble, or misstep, she strolled toward the church in a pair of stone-embellished platform heels. Her silky black Brazilian weave hung long and loose across her shoulders.

Skip, the building engineer and one of the deacons, opened the door for her and Baby Audrey. "Hello, First Lady."

"Hi, Skip. How are you this morning?" Detria flashed what could easily have been taken as a flirtatious smile. She raised up her free hand. "Don't answer that. I can see quite well," she added and then turned away. “Did Stiles, I mean Pastor Graham tell you about fixing up one of the new offices for me in the Children’s wing?”

“Yes, ma’am. He sure did, and I’ve done it.” Skip smiled. Skip and Brother Jones were two of Stiles’ trusted, and loyal friends, and both of them were also deacons at Holy Rock. Skip, single and considered handsome by most women, had women at Holy Rock practically throwing themselves at the Idris Elba lookalike. “I hope you like it,” he said as he walked a step ahead of her in the direction of what was to be her new home away from home.

Detria was pleasantly surprised when Skip opened the door to her brand new office space. She inhaled a whiff of his intoxicating cologne as she passed by him and stepped inside the comforting space.

She studied the newly decorated office. Two eye-popping bubble club chairs, a grape womb chair she’d ordered online, and a striking, dark finished mahogany desk with the perfect accessories, were exactly what she’d wanted.

“Audrey, look at mommy’s new office. We’re going to spend a lot of time here.”

“Would I be presumptuous if I said that your smile means you like what you see?” Skip commented.

“No you wouldn’t. And, I definitely like what I see,” she replied.

Skip blushed. Detria noticed.

She had great plans for her newly self-apprised role. She was about to let everyone know by her constant presence that her husband was off limits. There was only one queen bee at Holy Rock, and she was it.

She often told Brooke how sick and tired she was of women calling her house all times of day and night talking about they needed prayer, or somebody in their family is sick. *Let 'em pray for themselves. Stop calling my man,* she often thought. She felt like Holy Rock women were always up in her face, smiling and grinning, all the time wanting her husband. She was no naïve female; she was up on the game women in the church played.

While Stiles did his thing, she would be about doing her thing. Baby Audrey could stay in her office or go to the childcare center. If she had to use some of them to babysit Audrey while she exercised some freedom in her own life, so be it, because there was no way was she going to sit back and let one of them sneak up and grab her man from underneath her nose. She learned a lot from watching and listening to First Lady Audrey. One thing was certain, Audrey Graham made sure Pastor knew how much she adored him, and she was determined to do the same with Stiles. What better way than to work with him in the ministry.

"Skip, I love it," she said again after pulling herself from her thoughts. "The dark hardwood floors, the window treatments, the bookshelves. Oh, and my new desk. When did it get here?" she whirled around and found herself face to face with Skip's chest. "Oops, sorry about that." She apologized quickly.

Skip took a quick step backward. "Yesterday evening. So you like it, huh?"

"Absolutely. Thank you so much. You've made my office like my own private sanctuary," she said. Baby Audrey began to cry and her pacifier fell out of her mouth. Skip leaned down and picked it up.

"Don't cry, pretty girl," he told Baby Audrey. "I'll be right back. I'm going to go rinse this off." He turned to leave but Detria stopped him.

"Wait."

"Yes?"

"Where are you going? Remember, I have a bathroom in here. You can rinse it off in there." She laughed seductively and pointed toward the bathroom.

Skip responded with laugher of his own. "Yea, sure thing."

"Shhh, just hold on a minute, little girl. Mommy's going to feed you," she said in a soothing voice before focusing her attention back on Skip. She walked around her office and bounced Audrey on her hips. "Of course, I don't mind. If it wasn't for you, there's no telling how long I would have to wait for this office to be completed. Your friend, the Pastor," she emphasized seems to have more important things on his plate.

Skip responded by quietly going in the direction of the bathroom. A second or two later, he presented the pacifier to Baby Audrey who eyed it like she was insulted that he would present such a hideous thing to her. She was about to indulge in some real food, straight from her mommy's breast. A pacifier no longer interested her.

"Let me feed her, Skip. We'll talk soon," Detria said, and sat down in one of the two leather guest chairs. Before Skip could counter, or leave, she reached inside her dress and proceeded to expose her breast of which Baby Audrey quickly latched onto.

"Uh, okay. Let me let you get to taking care of that little princess," Skip replied like he'd been caught doing something he shouldn't, and in what may have been no more than two or three steps, he disappeared.

Detria smiled. "That's mommy's little girl," she whispered. "Right on cue. Yes you are definitely mommy's good, little girl."

5

"The only way love can last a lifetime is if it's unconditional. The truth is this: love is not determined by the one being loved but rather by the one choosing to love." Stephen Kendrick

Francesca and Tim returned to their spacious four-bedroom home after a seven-day stay at a place people called The Healing Place. Tim had been doing extensive research about AIDS ever since he became involved with Francesca. His research had paid off this time, he hoped when he learned about the Healing Place. There was supposed to be a natural herbs doctor near the village who reportedly said he could cure the disease. When he first told Francesca about it, she wasn't the least bit apprehensive, which surprised Tim. She was willing to try any and everything if it meant it would make her life better and possibly longer.

The journey was long and quite tedious for Francesca, but she endured it. The healing village staff gave her one on one attention and weren't the least bit turned off by her disease. They embraced her and Tim with unconditional love and genuine concern. The sanctuary was nestled in the hills of the coastal city of La Cieba, Honduras and was considered a tropical like haven; a place where Francesca could learn how to let go of old habits, and allow her body to go through a once in a lifetime revitalization process. She changed her diet drastically, staying away from all dairy, refined sugars, meat, fish and poultry among other things.

Tired from the return trip home, Francesca didn't waste a moment getting ready for bed. The trip to the Healing Place had been well worth it in Francesca's eyes. Combined with her faith, and her devoted husband, Francesca felt like she had the chance of living a full and healthy life.

Seven o'clock was early for Tim to call it a night, but he understood that his wife needed as much rest as possible. He put away their luggage and made sure Francesca was all right before he prepared himself a cup of herbal tea. He leafed through his Bible and read some of his favorite passages of scripture.

"Tim," Francesca called, yanking him from his time of meditation.

"I'm coming," Tim answered and hurried in the bedroom. "What is it?" he asked.

"What time are you coming to bed? You know how difficult it is for me to sleep when you're not lying next to me."

Tim smiled at his bride. The past two years had not been easy for either of them. Since their marriage, Francesca had been in and out of one hospital after another. It was nothing short of a miracle for her to even still be alive. She definitely had faced some scary, death harrowing moments. Living with AIDS was not easy and being the spouse of an AIDS victim was equally as difficult. Tim prayed that the products he bought home with him from Honduras would be the miracle from God he had been praying about for his wife.

Tim unbuttoned his shirt before he climbed on top of the bed sheets, and next to Francesca.

"Better?" he asked.

"Umhumm," she responded and snuggled in closer to her husband.

Francesca still couldn't quite grasp the fact that she was married. Living the life of a lesbian was all she'd known since she was fifteen years old, when she and Rena had their first intimate encounter. Francesca was actually shocked that Rena offered to appease her curiosity of what it would be like to be with someone of the same sex. It wasn't the same as when Fonda molested her as a young girl. It was a far cry from the way she felt back then; dirty, disgusting and scared out of her wits. Audrey, her own mother, who saw the nasty things Fonda made her do, not once did she try to protect her. No, instead she made Francesca believe it had been her fault, that she was the reason Fonda hurt her. What kind of mother was she, Francesca often asked herself. Other folks looked down on her for not being upset when Audrey died, but Francesca could care less. They didn't know her story; no one knew her story.

Francesca laid in Tim's arms, but her thoughts contemplated Rena. Stiles had told her that Rena was supposed to be getting married, or she had already gotten married. She couldn't remember which but she just wanted Rena to be happy. Yet, part of Francesca believed Rena could never be happy with any man because deep down inside Rena was in love with her. Rena could play the innocent one if she wanted to, and Francesca was fine with letting her play that fake role, but the bottom line remained, it was Rena who baited her in all those years ago to do what they did. She was the one who had been turned out, not Rena.

Rena was just a cleaner version of Fonda. No one would believe that because Rena always acted like she was so innocent and naïve. Francesca knew her like the back of her own hand, and she was not some poor, little victim. Maybe Stiles, Audrey, Pastor and even Rena's own parents believed that she was, but Francesca knew better.

Francesca smiled when she heard Tim's light snore. Tim was a good man. He adored her. *I wish I could love you the way you deserve to be loved. I wish I could turn back the hands of time, and then I wouldn't be living with this God-awful AIDS. Back then I would have fought off Minister Travis the night he raped me. I would have fought and screamed when Fonda molested me. I should have been stronger. And Rena. Why didn't I just tell her no when she said I could experiment on her? I didn't mean it for real. I was just talking. Why didn't she see that?*

Tears softly ran down Francesca's red cheeks as her past invaded her present. She hated the life she'd led. She hated being the victim over and over again. She hated that everyone who should have loved her, and protect her turned out to be the very ones that hurt her. She couldn't be the same with Tim. She may not have been in love with him, but she loved him for loving her.

She loved him because he saw past all of her past and he still wanted her. She owed him so much, and her plans were to never ever let him down.

"Tim. Tim, honey wake up." Francesca eased from next to him and sat upright in the bed.

"Hmm," he responded and sat up. "You need something, baby?"

"No, I'm good. Why don't you take the rest of your clothes off and get in the bed. You were snoring. I know you have to be tired too. You ran around Honduras practically nonstop, and the plane ride back was exhausting too." Francesca stroked the side of his face with the back of her hand.

"I'm fine," Tim said. "You hungry?"

"No. I'm good. Just concerned about you. Have you eaten anything?"

"A bowl of fruit. You want me to fix you some?"

"No, just want to make sure you're all right. Are you going to get in bed then?"

Tim got up and took off the rest of his clothes. "I'm going to take a shower. You wanna join me?"

"Sure. Then we can climb under the covers and spoon a little," she said with a smile on her face.

"Sounds good to me," Tim answered. He reached his long arm across the bed toward Francesca, and gently guided her out the bed and on to her feet. "Come on." He kissed her with unbridled passion until he heard a moan escape from Francesca's lips.

The warm water of the shower was soothing. She stood underneath the jet streams and she and Tim bathed each other. His touch always made her long for his lovemaking. It hadn't been like that when they first got married. It wasn't so much because she had AIDS that she was frightened about making love, because she insisted that Tim, even now, wear a condom. The thought that she could infect him, weighed heavily on her mind. Yet, Tim never made her feel uncomfortable about her disease. She was more afraid of not being able to respond to a man's touch. Tim was so sweet, so kind and easy to love that she wanted to do everything she could to assure his happiness, and that included being the best wife she could possibly be.

Their first time making love was awkward, but Tim was gentle, and didn't pressure her at all. That was another reason she loved him; the man was like someone out of a fairytale. She was totally into being all woman and enjoyed being treated like a lady.

"Why are you putting on a nightgown?" Tim asked. "I want to feel all of you lying next to me. No barriers," he said.

"Is that right?" Francesca threw the nightie to the side and climbed in the bed. She held the bed cover back for Tim to get in. He did.

He turned toward her. "I love you. I love you so much." His lips caressed hers while simultaneously he massaged her hips with his hands.

"I love you more," she said. "I love you more." Without warning, her mind betrayed her with thoughts of Rena. Why couldn't she get her off her mind? Rena was living her life, and Francesca wanted to live hers, at least what she thought she had left of it.

Her time spent at The Healing Place was beneficial in so many ways. She learned that by changing her total diet, she might be able to prolong her life expectancy from living a mere three years with AIDS to living as long as a person who was not infected. With her renewed faith, a good man by her side, and her new health regiment, Francesca was determined more than ever to live life to the fullest. Now if only she could keep thoughts of Rena at bay.

6

"It is not flesh and blood but the heart which makes us fathers and sons." Johann Schiller

Stiles parked in the space in front of Pastor's apartment home. He turned off the ignition and looked over his shoulder. "You are such a good girl. Such a daddy's little girl," he told Audrey.

He got out of the car and walked to the back passenger side door, opened it and with ease he removed Audrey from her car seat. He kissed her forehead, followed by each one of her chubby, rosy cheeks.

"Let's go see granddaddy. Okay?" Stiles continued to talk to his daughter as he walked toward his father's apartment.

"Knock on the door," he said and took Audrey's little hand, balled it into a baby fist and lightly tapped it on Pastor's front door. "You're so smart. If your grandmamma was still alive, she would have you spoiled rotten." Stiles grinned and then gave the door a harder knock. Within a few seconds, it swung open.

Before Stiles could say one word, Pastor had already focused all of his attention on Baby Audrey. He reached for her and willingly Audrey leaned out and over into Pastor's arms.

"Hey there, granddaddy's little angel. How is granddaddy's angel doing?" Pastor slowly walked into his living room with Audrey in his arms. He still showed some physical signs of his previous two strokes in the way he walked, like he was walking on eggshells.

Stiles closed the front door and followed Pastor. He took a seat on the small purple sectional, and Pastor sat down in his chair. Stiles watched as Pastor bounced Baby Audrey up and down on his knee. She giggled and clapped her hands awkwardly. Both men chuckled.

"You and my little angel out without her mommy?" Pastor asked without taking his eyes off the baby.

"Detria's at church meeting with volunteers and staff about the media blitz she's spearheading for the grand opening of the academy."

"I see," said Pastor. "Detria has really become active at the church hasn't she? Your mother would be proud of her. She's grown into an awesome first lady." Pastor stopped bouncing the baby. "It's a blessing she's serving in the ministry and supporting your vision for Holy Rock. Son, I'm proud of you. I'm proud of Detria. God is so good." Pastor turned away from Audrey and looked at Stiles.

"Thank you, Pastor, and you're right. God is good." Stiles pursed his lips and sighed.

"But?" Pastor asked.

"Well, don't get me wrong. I'm thankful that she wants to work more in the ministry. That's well and fine, but hey, don't be sniffing up under my butt, like she's trying to see what I'm doing."

Pastor shook his head. A faint smile formed on his face. "Son, you can't have it both ways. You want a woman, a helpmeet, someone who understands the call God placed on your life. You want a wife who is also a good mother. Detria seems to meet those qualifications." Baby Audrey touched Pastor's mustache and then she tried to gum it. Pastor laughed. "Oh, no you don't," he said to her in a gentle tone. "You're not using my mustache as your teething cookie."

"Pastor, look," Stiles lifted his hands. "I am not disputing any of what you've said. And, like I said, I'm grateful to God, but I'm also telling you that she's a little too close. I can't turn at home or at the church without her being right there. The whole purpose of her not going back to work was to be a full time mother to Baby Audrey, not to start a full time ministry at church. She used to complain about my long hours away from home, and here she is spending more and more time away from the baby. She might as well be back at work."

Pastor remained quiet with a pensive look.

"Look, I didn't come over here to mouth off about my marriage. I just hoped that Detria would be content with being a full time mother. I had plans on telling her not to ever go back to work." Stiles shrugged. "Anyway, enough of that." Baby Audrey shut down the conversation none too soon for Stiles, when she started to cry. "She's ready to eat. Let me run out to the car and get her diaper bag."

"Okay, son," Pastor replied and held Audrey up against his chest and started rocking her. "Shhh, it's okay, sweetheart. Daddy's gone to get your bottle." Audrey began to quiet down.

Stiles reappeared, and walked over to her. With lightning speed, she grabbed the bottle from his hand, placed its nipple in her mouth, and leaned back into Pastor's arms.

"Pastor, let's get to why I'm here."

"I know why you're here. You brought my angel here to see me."

"I know that, but you told me earlier this week that you wanted to talk to me about Emerald Estates. So tell me, what's going on? You want to move back there?"

Pastor cocked his head. "That would be nice, but not practical. I'm fine right here. The tenants are taking pretty good care of it. That's a blessing. Not too many people care as much about your stuff as you do. And the money I get in rent helps me out. God's favor." Pastor shook his head. "God's favor." He chuckled. Baby Audrey peered at him with wide eyes, never once taking her lips off her bottle.

"Okay, so what about Emerald Estates?"

"I still have a lot of things up in that attic. I've been thinking about what all is up there. A lot of papers, I know, some of my sermons, picture albums. " Pastor spoke slowly. "And mixed in with all of those items I'm sure is junk. Things that need to be gone through. Your mother used to do spring cleaning every year. I need to get back in the swing of things and pick up where she left off."

"I guess it is time to see if it's stuff we need to continue to keep or throw out."

Suddenly Pastor looked uncomfortable.

"What's wrong?" Stiles asked then concentrated his gaze on Audrey. She was making one of those I'm boo-booing faces. "Oh, sweetheart you need your diaper changed?" Stiles stood up, walked over, and removed his daughter from Pastor's lap.

"Oh, it's not the baby. She's fine. I just need you to get somebody to get that stuff out of the attic and bring it over here so I can go through it."

"No problem." Stiles paused. "Look, why don't I get it down and take it to my house? That way I can go through some of it for you, and whatever looks important, I'll put it aside and you can come over to my place and go through it," Stiles suggested.

"Yeah, that sounds good."

"That way you won't have to clutter your apartment with boxes," Stiles added.

"Thank you, son."

"No problem. I'm going to go back here and change the baby. I'll be right back."

"Sure," Pastor said and waved his hand.

Moments later, Stiles returned with a happy looking Audrey.

"That child knows she's adorable," Pastor said. "I sure hate that you feel like Detria is neglecting her motherly duties."

"I didn't say that she's neglecting the baby. It's just that she doesn't spend as much time with her the way I thought she would, or could. Now don't get me wrong, I love taking care of my daughter, but from what I've heard about parenting, it's the mother who makes all the difference in a child's life."

Pastor nodded.

Stiles leaned over and kissed her while she nestled in his arms. Her eyes drooped like they were heavy as a ton of bricks. Stiles kissed her on the top of her head. Baby Audrey didn't move. Her eyes remained closed in sleep this time.

"I think you know for yourself that Detria is not the perfect little wife. I mean, look how she did you, for God's sake. She beat you and treated you like crap when you were sick, when you couldn't speak for yourself, or defend yourself."

"Son, that's all in the past. And I forgave her, and so did you. Or so I thought. But it sounds like you still have some anger built up in you."

"It's not anger. It's just that sometimes I'm not sure about that woman."

"When she took her frustrations out on me, remember she was under a lot of pressure and strain. After all, the woman believed I was responsible for her miscarriage."

Stiles nodded. "Yea, sure she did."

"Look, I don't see what that has to do with anything we're talking about. So there's no need to talk about it anymore. I want to leave the past in the past."

Stiles tenderly gathered Audrey closer in his arms as he stood up. "It's almost three o'clock. I need to get home so I can get ready for Bible study this evening."

"What are you going to do about the baby?" Pastor asked.

"Detria is supposed to be home by four, no later than four-thirty, so she'll have the baby."

Pastor stood up and walked toward the door, stopping next to Stiles to pick up Audrey's diaper bag. I'll walk y'all out to the car. I'm sure glad you came over here. I feel relieved too that you're going to take care of cleaning that attic out."

"Yea, don't waste another second thinking about that. I'm going to get on it ASAP."

Father and son walked to the car. Baby Audrey didn't budge in the least when Stiles placed her in her car seat.

"She's out for the count," Pastor said, followed by a chuckle.

"That she is," Stiles answered, opened the driver's side of the car and climbed inside. "I'm glad me and Audrey got a chance to spend a little time with you today. I know I need to come by more often but—

"Don't." Pastor showed his palm. "Your wife and child need you, and Holy Rock requires your time and attention. Believe me, I know that it's hard work being the shepherd over a growing flock like yours. Shucks, it was hard enough for me when the church had barely 500 members. Now God has blessed so much that you have what – three, four thousand plus members?"

Stiles smiled proudly and nodded. "I am so glad to see how much God is moving at Holy Rock. People are coming, lives are being changed and with the new Children's Center and Holy Rock Academy opening next month, it's a lot going on, but I'm not complaining."

"You make me proud, son. You make me proud. Now take my precious little sleeping beauty home. I'll see you at Bible Study tonight."

Stiles closed the door, started the ignition, and drove off. "Lord, help me to be more grateful for my wife," he prayed out loud. "I don't want to be selfish, yet Father God, it's something warring in my spirit about her. Something just doesn't feel right."

Stiles stopped praying when he heard Baby Audrey's cries. "It's okay, honey. We'll be home in a few minutes, and daddy will get you out of that old car seat," he said softly. “But whether your momma will be there to greet us, is a horse of a different color.”

7

"When mistrust comes in, love goes out." Irish saying

Stiles looked at his iPhone again. It was almost six o'clock, and Detria still had not made it home. He tried calling her again, and once again, her phone went to voice mail. He called Holy Rock but no one answered. It was after hours, but he hoped that Skip would pick up, but he didn't.

Next, he fed Baby Audrey and afterward, he began to repack her diaper bag so he could take her with him. He could get one of the ladies at church to look after her while he taught, of that he was certain. But where in the world was Detria and why wasn't she answering her phone.

His anger fumed as another half hour came and went, and still no word from Detria. "Come on, sweetpea. Let's get outta here." He scooped up Baby Audrey out her crib, and headed downstairs when he

heard the door leading into the kitchen from the garage
made his way down the
rey.
ıe asked. His voice raised
ou and calling you. I even
ɔly." Stiles bit his bottom
have been more angrier

ːria said to Baby Audrey
Stiles. "Mommy missed
ıued.
where the heck have you

lanation, but I lost track
ɾying to get everything
mes next week. There's
nt the academy and the
... to be perfect.

Baby Audrey started to fuss. "Come on, darling." Baby Audrey leaned out of Stiles arms toward her mother. "That's my girl," Detria said in a sweet, motherly tone. She planted tiny kisses on each of Baby Audrey's cheeks.

"You couldn't answer your phone or return a text? Come on, tell that to somebody who'll believe it."

"I don't have to tell it to anybody, especially you. Anyway, I don't have time for this. I have to get a shower and change clothes."

Stiles looked stunned as he remained on the bottom step. "For what?"

"What do you mean, for what? Bible study, Pastor Graham," she said in a mocking tone.

"Oh no, you don't. You haven't spent any time with your baby all day. And it's not like you come to Bible study every week anyway. You're going to stay right here and see to my daughter. That's what you're going to do."

Detria rolled her eyes at her husband, and swiftly skirted pass him and up the stairs, holding Baby Audrey on her hip.

"Detria," Stiles said as she disappeared from his view. "You heard what I said," he yelled. "Take care of my daughter; I'll take care of what goes on at Holy Rock."

He heard her reply from upstairs. "You better go or you'll be late for your own Bible Study, Pastor," she yelled.

Stiles walked with force through the kitchen and toward the door leading to the garage. He opened the door and slammed it behind him.

◊

Stiles could barely maintain his composure from the pulpit as he taught Bible Study. He couldn't believe Detria had defied him by coming to church anyway, and to add fuel to the flame, Detria didn't have his daughter with her. He zeroed in on Detria, making eye contact with her. He could have sworn she had a big smirk on her face. Looking away before he lost his religion, as his mother used to say when she was about to go off on somebody, Stiles continued teaching.

"God will never leave you. God will never forsake you. No matter what you go through in life; God is able," Stiles told the sanctuary full of people. "He's Jehovah Jireh, your provider. If you need to be healed, He's Jehovah Rapha. Yes, people, God is a present help in time of trouble. He is Elohim, the almighty God."

People all over the 3,500 seat sanctuary, clapped and echoed words of praise. “He’s Jehovah Raah, our shepherd. He’s everything you need Him to be.”

For the remainder of the hour-long Bible Study, Stiles was consumed with teaching the word of God. He’d handle his problems with Detria when he got home.

At the end of Bible study, a majority of the congregation mixed and mingled. Many of them went to the front of the sanctuary to shake Stiles’s hand. Other surrounded themselves around Detria.

After fifteen minutes of nonstop handshaking, and “God bless you’s” the armor bearers escorted Stiles to the Pastor’s quarters, while another armor bearer escorted Detria out of the sanctuary.

“Where the hell is my daughter?” Stiles asked in a hushed tone when Detria walked into his office.

“My, my, my. The word of God is definitely true. From the same mouth come blessing and cursing. My husband, these things ought not to be so,” Detria mocked.

Stiles took a step toward her. “Don’t you try to stand here and quote scriptures to me. Just go get my daughter.” He looked around his office like he was checking to make sure there was no one in there with him and Detria.

Detria laughed.

“Where is my daughter, I said?” asked Stiles. A knock on the door cut him short, and he was glad for the interruption. He bit into his bottom lip like he could almost taste blood.

“Who is it?” he asked but Detria didn’t give the person on the other side of the door time enough to answer. She hurried to the door and opened it.

"Thank you so much, Mother Brown for taking care of our bundle of joy," she said with a pleasant smile on her face. She turned and looked at Stiles. "Honey, Mother Brown is such a blessing isn't she?" She gave Stiles a sideways smile as she removed Baby Audrey from the woman's arms.

Stiles cracked a fake smile. This argument was not over, not by a long shot. He walked up next to Detria. "God bless you, Mother Brown. Was she a good girl for you?"

"Oh, Pastor Graham, she was the perfect little angel. We had a good time together, didn't we Baby Audrey," Mother Brown said and patted the baby's balled fist. "She's been a good baby ever since she was born. And you know what Pastor Graham?"

"What, Mother Brown?" Stiles replied.

"She looks more like First Lady Audrey every day, God rest her soul." Mother Brown shook her head.

"Do you think so?" asked Detria. "I thought she looked more like my mother."

"Well, honey she does look like her too. Got your mother's nose, I'd say. But just looking at her, I see First Lady Audrey all over that child, even the way she looks at you."

Detria smiled and so did Stiles.

"Well, thank you again, Mother Brown. I didn't want to miss Bible Study, so I'm glad you agreed to watch her. You know, these days you have to be careful who you let look after your children. Folks are crazy, even in the church," Detria added.

"You sho' right, First Lady. But you don't have to worry about that. I'll always take good care of her."

"We know that, don't we Pastor Graham?" Detria turned and looked up at Stiles.

"Yes, yes," he stuttered. "We know. Mother Brown, you better get going. Deacon Brown is probably gathering his posse to come looking for you." Stiles smiled.

Mother Brown smiled in return. "I do need to get going. He's probably already outside in the parking lot waiting on me." She turned to leave. "And remember," she stopped and looked over her shoulder, "I've raised seven children of my own, and now I help take care of my grandchildren. So, one more won't be a bother especially when they're as good as Baby Audrey."

"Thank you, Mother Brown," Detria responded. "Have a blessed night," she said and closed the door when Mother Brown stepped out of the office.

Next, Detria whipped around with Baby Audrey on her hip, and clinging to her mommy's dress. "We're going home." Detria gathered the bag Mother Brown had set down on the table when she bought the baby in the office. "If you don't mind, stop at Déjà Vu Restaurant on your way home, pick up something for dinner. I have to get Audrey bathed and fed. And, it's been a long day. I do not feel like cooking." She opened the door and walked out, leaving a red-faced Stiles standing with his jaws on swoll.

When did this marriage go wrong? Or has it ever been right? Stiles rubbed his hand over his head and drove in the direction of the restaurant and home. Detria was trying him, and she was trying him real tough, but he couldn't figure out why. He thought after Baby Audrey was born, that their relationship would flourish. He was wrong. Dead wrong. Instead of being a happily married man, more and more he was turning into a miserable, unhappy married man. *God, I can't let this marriage fail too. But this is getting harder every day. Detria is changing right before my very eyes, and I don't know what to do about it. I don't know if I even want to do anything about it.*

Stiles arrived at Déjà Vu, a tiny little vegan restaurant on Florida Street in the heart of South Memphis. Detria told him about the restaurant a few months prior. Since their initial visit, Stiles and Detria ate their often.

Stiles ordered two spinach and mushroom quesadillas, and two additional side orders of sliced tomatoes and spring rolls to go. Back in his car, and on his way home, Stiles started thinking again about his life. How could he have possibly made another relationship mistake? What was wrong with him? First, it was Rena that betrayed him. And Detria, well Detria could have killed his father but yet he stayed with her. But why? Pastor may have forgiven her, but there were times Stiles still resented her for abusing Pastor. Stiles often prayed for Detria to be a good mother. He couldn't be responsible for what he might do if he she abused his daughter.

Rena, guess you're married or about to be married? Stiles looked at the date on the control panel of the car. *You're a better man than me, Robert.* Stiles switched from thought mode to talking out loud to himself as he drove. "I couldn't do it, man." *Couldn't stay with someone I couldn't trust.* Hope she's for real with you, because she definitely wasn't real with me."

Stiles walked into the kitchen with the bags of takeout. He sat the bags on the granite covered island countertop. He walked further into the kitchen on his way to the foyer area when he heard Detria talking on the phone.

"Let me call you back," he heard Detria say to someone obviously on the phone. " I can't. I told you he's home. Bye."

"Who was that?" Stiles asked when he walked up on her in the foyer.

"So now you want to monitor my phone calls? Tell me something, Stiles? Why the sudden jealousy? You've never been jealous, so what's up with all of the questions?"

"I said, who was on the phone?" Stiles said in a demanding voice.

Detria laughed, walked toward him, but sashayed pass him.

Stiles turned, and with quickness grabbed hold of her elbow, spinned her around until she faced him. He snatched the cell phone out of her hand and attempted to scroll through her phone, but it was password protected.

When they were first married, Stiles often made fun of how much she used to change the passwords on her phone, her emails, social media accounts, twitter all her other technology accounts. It was funny back then, but tonight it served only to push him to his limit, and without thought, he pushed her down to the floor, raised his hand back to strike her. Like God stilled the hand of Abraham when He was about to kill Isaac, Stiles' hand stopped in mid-air. His eyes gleamed.

Detria jumped up, her face full of tears she ran out of the room and bolted up the stairs.

Stiles heard a door slam. Immediately he felt partially ashamed of what he'd almost done. He covered his face with his hands. Hot tears streamed through his fingers. "God, help me. What is happening to me?"

Slowly, Stiles went upstairs. The bedroom door was closed. He walked down the hallway to Baby Audrey's nursery. She wasn't there. Turning he started back toward their bedroom, but as if pricked by a needle he stopped and went to his study instead. There Stiles buried his head in his hands as he thought about the anger that almost caused him to physically abuse Detria. She may have been smart mouthed and cocky but that gave him no right to strike out at her. After an hour passed, Stiles got from behind his desk and walked over to the leather sofa where he planned on sleeping for the night. He didn't know what to say to Detria just yet.

Stiles dozed off but was awakened over in the night by Baby Audrey's cries. He rubbed his eyes and sat up. Next to him in her portable crib, was his daughter. He looked around, still somewhat groggy and disoriented. No Detria.

"Come on, sweetpea. Daddy's got you." He lifted the fretting baby out of the crib and cradled her in his arms. He saw a bottle filled with milk propped in the corner of the crib. Stiles reached for it before he sat back down on the sofa. Audrey hungrily reached for the bottle and guided it into her own mouth. She laid back in her daddy's arms.

After Audrey finished her bottle, Stiles got up and took her to the nursery. He changed her pamper and rocked her to sleep in the rocking chair Detria had been excited to purchase for their baby, but now she rarely if ever used it. Audrey was asleep in minutes. Stiles laid her in her crib, covered her with her favorite pink blanket and then turned to leave.

"You could have just woke me up instead of leaving our daughter without telling me. Suppose I slept through her cries? What then?" he said when he walked into their bedroom. Detria was turned on her side. She didn't budge. Stiles didn't know if she was asleep or just ignoring him. He leaned toward the latter. "Detria, what is wrong with you? I know you hear me."

Detria pounced up like a lion. "Don't you come near me, Stiles. And I don't have to warn you when it comes to your child. She's just as much your responsibility as she is mine. I want you to get out of here anyway. I can't believe you hit me," she screamed. Stiles saw fresh tears pour from her eyes.

"I didn't hit you, Detria. And I'm sorry for raising my hand to you. I..I...I don't know what happened. I'm really, really sorry."

"Sorry isn't enough this time. You parade around the church and this community like you're so holy and righteous, unscathed. If only your church folk knew you like I know you. What would they think then? My momma always said if a man ever raises his hand to you once, he'll do it again and next time he'll use it. So you see, I'm not going to live in this house afraid of what you might do to me, or to my baby."

Stiles took a step toward their bed. "Don't bring up the church in this, Detria. This is between you and me." Stiles hit his chest with the flat of his hand. "And don't try to make this out to be all my fault. You still haven't told me who you were talking to on the phone. If that had been me hurrying to get off the phone like I had something to hide, you'd be flat out tripping. So don't even try it. I feel terrible that I allowed you to make me get that angry."

Detria pulled her knees up and pulled the cover up around her like she was shielding off the wind or something.

"I said, I want you out of here, Stiles. I mean it. If you don't leave right now, I'm calling the police," she threatened. "You can't tell me that just because I wouldn't tell you who I was talking to that I deserved to be physically abused," she yelled.

"What? Are you serious? Call the police for what? And what would you tell 'em, Detria? That my husband almost hit me three or four hours ago? Come on, now. We don't need the drama." Stiles eased over a little closer. "Let's talk this out." He offered, trying to calm his emotions.

"No, I do not want to talk to you. I just want you out of here." She picked up the house phone sitting on the nightstand next to their bed. "Now," she screamed again. "Or, I swear, I'm going to call 911."

His anger resurfaced and Stiles turned to leave the room. His nostrils flared. He slammed the door behind him. Stiles shook his head. This time he went to their guest room. He didn't bother getting out of his clothes. He kicked off his shoes and laid across the queen-sized four poster bed.

Unable to rest, Stiles sat up on the side of the bed. He saw the Bible opened and laying on the round table next to the bed. They had an open Bible in every room of their eleven room house. Stiles got the Bible and began reading the scripture. "Put on then, as God's chosen ones, holy and beloved, compassionate hearts, kindness, humility, meekness, and patience, bearing with one another...as the Lord has forgiven you, so you also must forgive." He stopped reading and put the Bible back on the table. "God why do I have to be the one who always has to do the forgiving? I know I'm called to be your messenger, Father. But I'm human too, Father. I'm sick and tired of being the one to turn the other cheek. I turned the other cheek when it came to Rena and my sister. I turned the other cheek when my mother betrayed our family. I turned the other cheek when my wife beat up on my father. And now, you expect me to turn the other cheek again, even though my wife blatantly disrespects me and neglects my baby? What do you want from me?" Stiles cried out and then fell to his knees sobbing. "What do you want?"

8

"The hardest thing to learn in life is which bridge to cross and which to burn." David Russell

Rena and her sister, Delores left the final meeting with the caterer. Everything was set. The wedding was less than twenty-four hours away.

"Are you excited?" her sister asked.

"Of course, I'm excited. Why wouldn't I be. I'm about to marry a wonderful man who adores me and loves me for who I am. And his kids love me too." The two sisters got in the car and drove in the direction of their parents' home.

"Look, Rena I'm your sister. And I'm eleven years older than you, so I know a few things," she laughed, and glanced over at Rena before turning her eyes back to the rode. "And I know enough about you, little sis to see that you aren't as thrilled as a new bride should be. I'm just going to come out and ask."

"Ask what?" said Rena.

"Are you having second thoughts about marrying Robert?"

Rena looked at her sister who had her eyes glued to the street as she drove and talked. "Second thoughts? Where is all of this coming from?"

"I told you. I know you, Rena. And you are not the happy little bride. Tell me, and I promise this won't go outside of this car. You haven't gotten over Stiles have you?"

"Don't be ridiculous, Delores. It's been four years since Stiles and I divorced. He's remarried and gone on with his life."

"You haven't answered my question? Are you still in love with him?"

Rena gave pause. "Look, I am not in love with Stiles. Do you think I would be marrying Robert if I was in love with my ex? I don't think so."

"People do it every day, so you wouldn't be the first one. All I want for you is happiness. I don't know the details of why you and Stiles got divorced and I don't need to know. But I don't want to see you compounding your mistakes either. Just because Robert is a great guy and all, doesn't mean he's the man for you. That's all I'm saying."

"I'm getting married because I want to get married. I do not want Stiles Graham. And why would you think I'd want somebody who couldn't forgive me for my past mistakes? I don't care how much he gets up in the pulpit every Sunday preaching forgiveness, when it came to home, he couldn't forgive me." Rena turned her face toward the window.

"Look, I didn't mean to upset you. I just want you to be happy. And one last thing and then I'm going to be quiet about this whole thing. I don't know what you did and like I said I'm not trying to get all into the reason for your breakup with him, but the fact remains not one time have I heard you say you're marrying Robert because you love him."

Rena turned and faced Delores again. "You want to hear me say it, then I love Robert. Now are you satisfied?" she asked.

"Are you satisfied, is the question? I'm through with it." Delores raised one hand off the steering wheel and waved it in front of Rena's face. "It's your life. If you say you're happy, then I'm happy. Now enough of that. Do you still want to stop by Joe's Fish Seafood?"

"Umm, I guess so. I do still have a taste for some grilled cod, and they have the best."

"Okay, Joe's Fish it is," said Delores.

◊

"You know it's bad luck for the bride and groom to see each other before the wedding," Rena told Robert over the phone.

"It's not our wedding day yet. That's when it's bad luck. It's the night before the wedding, so why can't I come over there and spend a couple of hours with my bride-to-be," Robert pleaded.

"I've been running all day long. I'm tired, honey. I just took a hot shower and now all I want to do is crash." Rena yawned in the phone and curled up on her living room sofa.

"Okay, I guess I'll have to wait. But I don't like it. I want to be there, right next to you. These last few days have been torture."

"Come on now, Robert. It hasn't been that bad."

"Speak for yourself. It's hard enough not being able to make love to you for the past month, and now I can't come and see the woman I love the night before we say I do. I think that's a bummer, a real bummer."

"We'll have the rest of our lives to be together. And as for not making love, we both agreed, if you recall," she emphasized, "that we were going to abstain from sex until after we were married."

"You're the one who came up with that idea. I had no choice but to agree. You had already made up in your mind that you wanted us to stop having sex, for what I don't know. It would be something else if we had never been intimate with one another, but we have. So why the big cut-off," Robert questioned.

"Look, I am not going to go back through this with you, Robert Becton. So, why don't you watch a ball game or something and tomorrow will be here before you know it."

Rena heard a knock at the front door.

"Robert, someone's at the door. It's probably Delores. She went over to mom and dad's after we came back from the caterer."

Rena got up and walked toward the door. She peeped through the peephole and sure enough it was Delores with a big basket of something in her hands.

"Okay, baby. It *is* Delores, and she has a basket of, well I don't know what it is, in her hands. Let me help her. I'll talk to you tomorrow."

Robert sighed into the phone. "I love you, sweetheart."

"By, baby. See you at the church tomorrow," Rena told him and ended the call.

She opened the door and reached out to help Delores with not one basket but two."

"These are absolutely gorgeous," Rena said taking one of the baskets out of Delores's arms.

"Thanks. I thought I was about to drop one of them. Mama's Silver Sneakers exercise group made these. One is for you and the other one is for your step kids. Wasn't that thoughtful of them?" Delores added.

"Ohhh, yes." Rena closed the door behind Delores and the two of them walked into the dining room and placed the baskets on the table. Rena looked closely at the basket for her. It had lavender and citrus bath balls, foaming bath powder, a body net, a cotton waffle loofah mitt, lavender soy candles, lotion and several other items Rena couldn't make out."

"Girl, it smells so good doesn't it?" said Delores. "They really did a good job on these."

"Yeah, they did. I'm going to really enjoy using this stuff." Rena then looked at the one they had made for Robert's kids. "Oooh, look Delores. This one has crackers, cheese, cookies, chocolate, brownie bites, nuts and looks like a gift card of some kind. These are so sweet."

"They sure are. Girl, you are so blessed. You have so many gifts already. And wait until the wedding tomorrow. I know you and Robert are going to get tons more."

"I'm about to cry."

"Don't you start, Rena. Save those happy tears for the wedding. Oh, I almost forgot," Delores said.

"Forgot what?" asked Rena.

"Wait, let me run back out to the car and get it. Mama said FedEx delivered it earlier today," Delores explained as she headed back toward the front door.

She returned moments later with a small brown box in her hand and passed it over to Rena.

Rena studied the box like she was expecting something to magically appear.

"Well, are you going to open it?" Delores asked.

"Yes, I guess." Rena eyed the package again. "It's...it's from Memphis." Rena's face turned crimson red.

"Do you think it's from Stiles?"

"I don't know. But I'm about to find out." Rena reached for an ink pen off the table and used it as a knife to slit the tape and open the box. Inside the box was another box. This one was white and had a beautiful red ribbon wrapped around it.

"Who is it from?" Delores asked impatiently.

"Hold up." Rena looked around the inside of the brown box to see if there was a note card or tag. But deep inside she believed that it was from Stiles. She didn't recognize the address, She stopped searching for a name tag and proceeded to open the box while she tried to keep her hands from shaking. She pulled the ribbon and clumsily pulled off the top of the box. Paper covered whatever the gift was inside. She removed the paper and almost fainted when she picked up the package inside.

"Oh my gosh," Delores cried and placed her hand over her opened mouth. "Who would do something like this? Rena give it here," she ordered and removed the box of condoms from out of Rena's frozen hand. There was another one lying in the box that was out of the packet; it looked like it had been used.

Rena's mouth was still open. One hand held the package of condoms and the other hand held the lip of the box. She didn't focus on Delores removing the package from her hand. Rena stumbled over to the couch and fell back on it. Tears started flowing.

"Rena, this has to be some kind of gag gift. There's no need to get upset. We just overreacted. But whoever sent it," Delores said then paused and peaked inside the brown box. This time she pulled out a small white envelope. "Here, here it is. See who it's from."

Rena looked slowly over at her sister. She wiped the tears away with the back of her hand. "Give it to me," she said softly and reached for the envelope. Delores passed it to her and then stood positioned across from Rena with each arm folded inside the other one.

Rena opened the envelope and pulled out the card inside. *Don't spoil your wedding night AGAIN. Play it safe and keep him strapped up. Safe sex is the best sex. Oops, don't think you know anything about that,* the card read, but wasn't signed by anyone.

"What does it say?" Delores asked, her eyes as huge as rocks as she eyed the condoms.

"I don't want to talk about it." Rena began to tear up.

"Is it from Stiles?" asked Delores.

Rena shook her head.

"That low down dog. And he calls himself a preacher? How could he be so mean?"

"Did you hear me say it was from Stiles?" barked Rena as anger formed in the base of her tummy. "Look, I don't mean to be short with you, but I need to be alone right now." Rena stood up, wobbled a little and then steadied herself. "I'm going to my room. Please, make yourself at home," she said to Delores.

"Sure. Sure I understand. And I'll clean up this stuff. You just try to get some rest. You have a huge day tomorrow, and please, Rena. Don't let this spoil your wedding day. It's nothing more than a trick of the enemy to get you to thinking all crazy in the head. Don't fall for it."

Rena nodded. She left the package of condoms on the table along with the gift box that had the used condom in it, and disappeared down the hall.

She sat on the bedroom bench at the foot of her bed and cried. *How could he? All the time pretending he still cared about me. I should have known.* Rena toyed with the card she still held in her hand. She didn't know why she wanted to torture herself, but she flipped it over and read the message again. Then she saw it. How could she have missed it the first time? Maybe because she was too shocked at what was in the box and what the message said: "Wedding Wishes to the Bride and Groom from Pastor and First Lady Graham," Rena read then she lifted her head as thoughts rushed through her mind. "Lord, oh, Lord," Rena cried.

"Sis. Hey, sis. Are you okay in there?" Rena heard Delores ask from the other side of the bedroom door.

"Yes. I'm fine. I'll be all right." Rena tried to reassure her.

"Rena, please don't be upset. Try to let it roll off of you. You're going to be Mrs. Robert Becton this time tomorrow. Don't let this ruin your day."

"I hear you. And I said I'm all right. Don't worry," Rena told her without moving from the bench. "Towels, toiletries, whatever is all in the on-suite in the guest room. Help yourself to whatever you need," she told Delores.

"Yea, okay. But let me know if you need me. I'm going to the guest room."

"Thanks. Goodnight," she told Delores.

Rena looked at the card and read its message over and over again. She said continuously, "Pastor and First

Lady Graham," and then she seemed to hear something or someone say, 'be sure your sin will find you out.'"

9

"He who angers you conquers you." Elizabeth Kenny

Stiles left the house before Detria or Baby Audrey woke up. He had to get out of that place to clear his head after last night's events. He called Skip and asked him to meet him at the Blue Plate Cafe on Poplar for breakfast. Skip agreed.

The hostess greeted Stiles with a wide smile when he entered the Blue Plate.

"Good morning, sir. How many in your party?" she asked.

"Two. If you have a booth, I'd prefer that."

"Sure, follow me." She picked up two menus from behind the back of the booth and proceeded into the dining area of the restaurant, which was known for its delicious breakfast menu. She seated Stiles in a booth toward the front of the restaurant and next to the window facing the parking lot. "How is this?" she asked.

"This is fine."

"Your server will be right with you," the hostess said and then turned and left.

Stiles ordered a carafe of orange juice and a carafe of coffee and waited on Skip to arrive. Skip lived in the area, so it wouldn't be long before he arrived.

Ten minutes later, and nursing his second cup of coffee, Stiles glanced to the side, and saw Skip making his way to the table.

"Good morning, Pastor. What's got you up and out this early? Especially on a Saturday morning. I thought you'd be home enjoying that sweet little girl of yours."

"Normally, I would. But things got a little heated on the home front. I had to get out of there for a minute, man," he said to Skip.

"What's up? You and Detria had a little spat? Man, you see why I choose to remain single? Too much drama with being married."

"Man, I don't know what's up with that woman. Last night I come in and here her on the phone. She was telling somebody she had to hurry up and get off because I had just walked in. What kind of mess is that? You know she wouldn't be telling another female that."

Skip poured himself a glass of orange juice, his favorite, and proceeded to take two large gulps. He refilled his glass and this time he took a regular swallow. "You know she's not messing off on you. Don't even think that."

"I don't know what to think. I know it didn't sound right. And to make it worse, when I confronted her about it, she had the nerve to brush me off like I'm some Joe Blow on the street or something." Stiles pounded his chest. "Man, I'm her husband. I'm not going to let her treat me like I'm some fly by night dude or something." Stiles's temples beat like heartbeats against his smooth brown skin.

"You mean to tell me she did it like that? Wow, man that's messed up for real."

"Tell me about it. But that's not all. Skip, for the first time in my life, I lost it. I really lost it." Stiles sipped on his coffee and rubbed his forehead nervously.

"What do you mean, you lost it?" asked Skip.

"Man, I raised my hand to slap the..."

"You what?" Skip raised his voice and then just as quickly lowered it.

Stiles showed his palms. "No, I didn't hit her. I said I almost hit her but God stilled my hand. It was awful. You can imagine how things went from there."

Skip nodded. "She put you out?"

"Just about. She told me to leave. I tried to apologize and everything, but she wasn't hearing it. She even threatened to call the police. And I ended up sleeping in one of the guest rooms."

The server walked up, and momentarily interrupted their conversation to take their food orders.

"Well, you know I'm not one for hitting women," Skip said after the server left. "And I know you aren't either, so she must have really gotten next to you, bro."

"I'm telling you, all I could think about was what I went through with Rena. I don't want to go down that road again." Stiles shook his head and then took another sip of his coffee. "I'm telling you, Skip if this marriage crumbles, that's it for me. I'm going to be a certified bachelor. I don't care if I am a pastor, I'll just have to fight off the women as they come." Stiles laughed at his own remark.

Skip chuckled. “You won’t be bored, that’s for sure. I know I’m not. I enjoy the females at the church and out of the church. And Pastor, I’m just telling you from a friend aspect, you’ll have your choice of any woman you want when you’re free and single.”

Stiles tilted his head. “Are you serious, Skip? Are you suggesting that I should mess around on my wife?”

“Naw, man. I said if your marriage failed. But let’s not even think like that. You and Detria are bound to have disagreements, but you know that. So, this was a pretty huge spat, so what. Things will get right. You got yourself a good lady. Give her some time to cool off. Send her some flowers or send her to the spa for a day. Whatever you do. Just do something to get things back on track.”

“Yeah, you’re right. But still I want to know who she was talking to that she had to hurry up and get off the phone.”

“Forget that. If you go looking for trouble, you know what they say; you’re going to find it.”

Stiles nodded again. “That’s true.”

The server returned with their food. Both gentleman ate, and no further mention was made about Stiles’ marital woes.

“What you got up after this?” asked Skip. He scooped up a spoonful of grits and picked up a slice of bacon and put it in his mouth.

“I have to go to Emerald Estates. I promised Pastor that I would go up in the attic and take down some boxes he wants from up there.”

“Well, my schedule is free until around five. I’m going to the Grizzlies game this evening, but I don’t mind helping you out up until then.”

"Yeah, that'll be cool. I don't remember how much is up there, so any help I can get will be appreciated."

Stiles and Skip finished breakfast and left the restaurant headed in the direction of Emerald Estates.

Stiles drove down Elvis Presley Boulevard and decided to call Detria. The house phone rang until the voicemail came on. He ended the call and called her cell phone. Still no answer. "See this is the kind of mess I'm talking about. Lord, why does this woman keep trying me?" He hit his hand on the steering wheel and increased his speed. When he arrived at Emerald Estates, he parked in front of the house and waited until he saw Skip drive up and park behind him. Stiles got out of the car and stood in front of it.

Skip got out of his truck, his phone glued to his ear. "Hey, I'm at my destination. I'll hit you up when I leave from here. All right?" Stiles heard him tell whoever it was he was talking to on the phone.

"You ready to do this, man?" Skip asked as he walked up next to Stiles.

"As ready as I'm ever going to be." His nostrils flared with fury.

"What's up?" Skip asked as the two of them walked up the driveway toward the house.

"On the way over here, I tried to call Detria. I called on the house phone and the cell phone. She didn't answer."

Skip stopped walking. "Hold up, I think you're reading way too much into this. You know she's probably still heated, or she may just be busy seeing to the baby. Don't start letting your imagination run away with you."

Stiles rubbed his head back and forth. "I'm just saying. She could have easily picked up the phone and said she was busy with the baby. Something. But not to answer, and then she hasn't bothered to call back. I'm telling you, Skip, I gotta feeling that something's up with her."

"Man, she's always at the church, so I don't see how she has time to be messing off if that's what you're thinking. You got yourself a good woman, I'm telling you, man. Don't mess this up because you happen to be insecure because of your past. Where's your faith?"

Stiles rang the doorbell without bothering to respond to Skip's comments. They were welcomed inside by one of the tenants who told Stiles to take as much time as he needed.

For the next two plus hours, Stiles and Skip sorted through the neat maze of boxes, a couple of trunks, bedding, photo albums, an antique radio, all things from the Graham family. Their past was all more than likely nestled inside these boxes, most which he thought had probably been in the attic since he was a little boy. The more he looked through the things; some of his mother's personal items, costume jewelry, clothing that Stiles didn't know Pastor still had, the more engrossed Stiles became. He got carried into a world of his past, forgetting that he was not alone, but had bought Skip with him.

There was no telling how much history was in this attic. Stiles didn't recall seeing all of this when he put things up in the attic after Pastor moved out. Probably because he was still grieving over Audrey's death.

"Hey, man, are you about done?" asked Skip. "It's about that time for me. Need to get back on the other end, get ready for this game. "

"Naw, I'm finished. The boxes over near the stairs, that's what I'm taking. If you can help me get them down, I'm out of here too."

"Okay, let's do it," Skip said and headed in the direction of the four storage boxes.

They got the boxes inside Stiles' car. Skip left while Stiles drove off contemplating whether to go home or stop by Holy Rock. He ultimately decided to do neither, choosing rather to ride downtown and walk the trails on Mud Island.

Stiles looked up in toward the sky. It was a perfect summer day; mid-sixties. Blue skies. The sweet smell of bloomed flowers darted across the air above and around Stiles. Dogs running, barking. People walking, talking. Serenity filled Stiles from within. He exhaled.

"Lord, I praise you in the midst of my trial. Forgive me, father for my actions last night toward the woman you bought into my life. Help me to be a better husband and father." Stiles walked three miles around the trail before he returned to his vehicle and headed home.

On the way home, he stopped by one of Detria's favorite Chinese restaurants. She loved their vegetable fried rice and their freshly squeezed lemonade. Stiles wasn't sure if he would need Mother Brown, but he decided to call her just in case things turned out positively like he hoped they would when he talked to Detria. The two of them could have a little making up time and Audrey would be in a safe place so neither of them would have to worry.

He called Mother Brown. She told him she was available if he needed her. *So far, so good.*

Stiles smiled, turned up the radio, and song along with Bishop Paul Morton. *I'll pray for youuuu, you pray for me, watch God change things."*

10

"Everyone is like a moon, and has a dark side which he never shows to anybody." Mark Twain

Stiles pushed the remote and the garage door opened. It was empty of Detria's car. Stiles exhaled as he drove up in the garage, and flipped the remote at the same time he turned off the ignition.

"Dang, Detria. Where are you?" he said aloud. He got out of his car and entered into the kitchen from the garage. The aroma of fresh cooked food wafted pass his nose as he walked over to the countertop and opened the microwave to place Detria's food inside, but saw a plate of food already in the microwave. He removed the plate of green vegetables, corn, blackened tilapia and a corn muffin and put Detria's food inside.

"Guess this is for me." Stiles washed his hands at the island sink and then prepared to sit down at the table to eat. He looked around the kitchen as he enjoyed the delicious food. Detria had always been a great cook who believed in eating healthy.

He tried calling Detria again on her cell phone. This time she answered.

"Hello," she said dryly.

"I take it the food in the microwave was for me," he said.

"Don't I always leave your food in the microwave? So why would you think any differently?"

"I didn't say I thought any differently. I just wasn't sure. I didn't know if you were still angry with me or not."

Detria remained quiet.

"Hello," Stiles said. "You still there?" he asked.

"Yes."

"Where are you?"

"At the church." Her answers were short and to the point.

Stiles knew that she was still mad at him, but he felt he had every right to be mad at her too, but decided not to show his attitude. Instead he believed it was his duty to keep the peace in their household. If this marriage was going to work, he had to give in a little more.

"You must be getting things finalized for tomorrow's official opening of the Children's Center."

Detria's voice changed from bland to excitement as she talked about the activities she had planned to take place during eleven o'clock worship service and following the church services.

"The media will be here most of the day and the children are practicing as we speak in their new state of the art children's worship center. Stiles, everything is going to be perfect."

"I'm glad, sweetheart." He called her sweetheart without realizing it. " Detria, I want to tell you again how sorry I am about last night. I would never ever hurt you, let alone hit you. I guess I've been stressed out more than usual. You know with this new addition to the church, the opening of the academy and just the way Holy Rock is growing. It's a bit overwhelming. Tell me that you forgive me."

"Stiles, I forgive you, but it's just that last night, well I still can't believe how close you came to hurting me. I never thought I would be afraid of my own husband, but you. I don't know, Stiles. It was just plain scary."

"I know it was, and I promise you it'll never happen again. I've prayed and asked God to forgive me. I just got so crazy mad when I heard you on the phone. For a minute, all I could think about was what I'd gone through with Rena. I know all of that is in my past, but every now and then, I guess it still bothers me," he explained.

"I'm not Rena. I'm not your ex. And if you don't trust me, then what do we have?" she asked.

"You're right." Stiles took another bite of his food. "Look, we can talk about this later when you get home. I'm just glad you're talking to me again."

"Yea, sure, we'll talk later."

"Hey, where's my sweetpea?" .

"She's right here in the office with me. She's asleep on the sofa."

"Kiss her for me."

"I will."

Stiles thought he heard a man's voice in the background but he couldn't quite make out what the guy was saying to Detria.

"Is someone in your office with you?"

"Oh, that was Skip. He just walked in."

"Oh, that was quick."

"What was quick?"

"Well, I just left him. We had breakfast together, earlier, and afterward he went to Emerald Estates with me and helped me take some boxes down from the attic. Pastor said he wanted to go through some of that stuff and clear it out as much as possible. But anyway, Skip said he was going home and get ready for the game tonight."

"I called him and he told me the same thing, but I really needed him to come by and sign off on the work the subcontractors were finishing up this evening. I thought they were going to be finished yesterday, but you know how things go."

"Pastor, everything is in order. I'm about to get out of here." Stiles heard Skip tell him in the background.

"Tell him I hear him. And as for you, I guess I'll see you when you get home."

"Yea. Sure."

"Detria. Hold up."

"What?" she answered.

"I went by Pho Binh and picked up some fried rice." He could tell Detria was smiling by the tone of her voice.

"Oh, Stiles. Thank you. I'll have it for supper this evening. I put away a plate of food in the refrigerator for myself, but you can eat it."

"Cool. Talk to you later."

"Bye."

Stiles ate the remainder of food and felt some relief that the tension between him and Detria seemed to have passed. He had to be more disciplined when it came to his marriage and how he treated her. She was right; if there was no trust between them, there was no marriage.

After he finished eating, Stiles washed out his dishes and then retreated to the garage to get the boxes he'd bought home. One by one he removed each one and carried them into the downstairs room that used to be Pastor's bedroom.

"Might as well tackle some of this stuff," he said and sat down on the floor, pulling one of the boxes next to him. He opened the first box and sorted through the items. Most of the things were foreign to him so he put them aside for Pastor to look through. By the time he made it to the third box, Stiles was ready to call it quits until he saw a bright red cigar looking box. He removed it and opened it. Several documents were folded inside. One by one Stiles unfolded them. His mouth dropped open as he read what appeared to be letters exchanged between Pastor and Audrey. One of them caused Stiles' head to literally swim.

I cannot do this anymore. Every time I look at her, I hate her more and more. I did what you said, and I didn't have an abortion. But knowing that this, this child is unwanted....

"Who is she talking about?" Stiles asked himself. He wanted to put down the letter, put it back in the little red box but he couldn't. He understood that this was Pastor's personal belongings, but his curiosity kept his eyes glued to the words on the paper written in his mother's handwriting.

You're the one who wanted her. Why? Why wouldn't you just let me give her away? Or have an abortion. Oh, but you said abortion was murder. But I guess it was fine for me to go through all this torment over the years. Every time I look at her, I have to be reminded of that night. I have to live with it by looking at his baby every day of my life.

Sweat formed on Stiles' brow. He read the remainder of the letter. At the end it was signed *Audrey*.

"Is she talking about Francesca? No, no, no, she can't be," he told himself. He looked through the rest of the box. There were several news clippings paper-clipped together. One heading read, "Serial Rapist Prowling East Memphis Neighborhood". Hands shaking, Stiles skimmed over the rest of the clipping before he turned to a second one, then a third one, all talking about a serial rapist in East Memphis.

"I remember living in East Memphis before we moved to Emerald Estates," he said.

The fourth clipping read, '*Police have arrested a 27 year old convicted rapist who allegedly broke into two dozen homes in East Memphis over the course of six months. He entered the homes through a bedroom window, tied up his victims and forced them to disrobe at knifepoint...*

Detective Taurus Withers said each of the seven victims told investigators similar stories of a man armed with a jagged edge knife that came in through their bedroom window and sexually assaulted them.

The last headline read, *"East Memphis Serial Rapist Will Serve Life Behind Bars"*

Stiles returned the letter and the news clippings back to the red box. He picked up the box, stood to his feet and left the house. He had to find out who Audrey had been talking about in that letter. Was the man in the news clippings Francesca's father, or did he have another sister out there somewhere? A sister who was the product of rape? Audrey was dead, so Pastor was the only one who could give him the answers he needed, and Stiles was going to make sure that Pastor did just that.

11

"Of all the worldly passions, lust is the most intense. All other worldly passions seem to follow in its train."
Buddha

"What did he want?" asked Skip.

"Nothing. Trying to check up on me on the sly. And he's s trying to act all sweet now, hoping I'm not mad at him anymore."

"Are you?"

"I am not going to stand for any man hitting on me."

"But he didn't hit you, Detria. That's what you said."

"I don't care; he was about to. And he always wants folks to think that he's so holy and righteous. Skip, he may be your friend and your pastor, and he may be my husband, but I'm not the one. I don't deserve to be mistreated. And I will not be abused. I gave him a child, a beautiful daughter, and I'll be darned if he's going to flip out and act a fool just because I won't let him control me." Detria folded both hands together and leaned back in her office chair.

Skip smiled at her. "You are a firecracker, you know that?"

Detria responded with a flashy smile of her own. "Thought you had a game to go to," she said, still smiling.

"I do. That is," he paused. "Are we done here? Anything else you need?"

"Don't make me go there, Skip Madison." Resting her chin on her hand, she grinned mischievously. "Remember, I'm a married woman, and, the First Lady of Holy Rock." A smirk came across her face.

"Must you remind me," he murmured and turned to leave. "I'll talk to you later."

"Okay. Enjoy the game," she said.

"Thanks. I'll try to hit you up later, after it's over."

Detria nodded and watched Skip as he left, closing the door to her office. She got up, smoothed her fitted skirt, walked from behind her desk and went to the sofa where Baby Audrey still lay sleeping. She looked down at her, smiled and then turned and walked away while saying, "No wonder you don't sleep all night; you sleep all day."

Detria began tidying up her office, putting away Audrey's toys that she kept in the office, and her baby blanket. Looking inside of the diaper bag, she didn't see her pacifier. Detria searched around the office before she went in the bathroom to see if perhaps she'd left it in there; and she had. She retrieved it and put it in the bag, then put the bag on her shoulder. As she passed her desk, she grabbed her Chanel bag, and then went and picked up Audrey from off the couch. Audrey lifted her head, and looked around.

"You awake, little girl? Did Mommy wake you from your beauty rest? That's all right. You're going to always be beautiful no matter what," she told a sleepy looking Baby Audrey.

Detria locked the door to her office, and walked through the Children's Center a final time before she left Holy Rock for home. On her drive she thought about Rena and laughed a wicked laugh. "Audrey, your grandmother would be proud of me. That little lesbo slut. Your daddy and her think they could fool me, but never in this lifetime. Honey, one thing you're learn about your mother, is that it's hard to make a fool out of me. I know she still loves him. She probably still loves your Aunt Francesca too. And if I was any other woman, she'd probably have stolen your daddy right from under my nose. But," Detria raised one finger in the air as she drove and talked. "But, I'm not just any other woman. That's where she has me messed up. I bet she spazzed out when she opened that box." She chuckled loudly. "I know she's going to call him, and that's when I'm going to bust his tail." She glanced over her shoulder and quickly eyed Baby Audrey who was kicking her legs and sucking contently on her pacifier. "If he confronts me about something she told him, then I'm going to know that first, they have probably never stopped communicating, and two, I'll know where his heart is if he tries to go off on me about some other female, especially his ex. But we'll see, sweetpea. Won't we now?"

Detria pushed the power button on the steering wheel and the radio popped on. Immediately she turned up the volume and began to sing along with Kirk Franklin. *"After a while, after a while, this too shall pass...."*

◊

As Stiles approached Pastor's gated complex, he dialed his number to let him know that he was coming to pay him a visit. Stiles parked his automobile, grabbed hold to the red box and ran up the walkway.

Pastor answered the door. "Hello, son. To what do I owe this surprising visit tonight?"

"I did what you asked me to do. I cleared the attic, got rid of some stuff that I knew was of no value or importance to you. And I bought some boxes home with me. I started going through some of them."

Pastor patted Stiles on the shoulder as Stiles walked further into the apartment. Pastor closed the door.

"Thank you, thank you." Pastor said. "I'll get over there one day this week and go through some of the stuff you kept down."

Stiles raised the red box and pushed it out toward Pastor. "Tell me if you know what this is."

Pastor looked at the box and slowly regarded it. Stiles saw a disturbing frown form on Pastor's face.

"What are you doing with that?" Pastor asked. "Give it here. That was your mother's."

"So, you know what's inside?" Stiles watched Pastor as he turned and walked over to his recliner and sat down. His face suddenly looked like he'd age ten or fifteen years in a matter of seconds.

"Why is that of importance to you? Just give it here," Pastor said again in a demanding tone. "You had no right to go through her things. I told you I would do that."

"And I told you that I was going to sort through some of the things first, so it wouldn't be so much on you. I just didn't have any idea that I would find out a shameful, dirty family secret."

"It's none of your business. I don't care what you saw or read."

"So you do know what's inside this box, don't you? And everything my mother has gone through when she was here on this earth, you're responsible for it," Stiles yelled. "Tell me, father," Stiles said in a disrespectful tone. "Who is my mother talking about? Where is this child you made her have because of your religiosity?"

"I don't owe you an explanation about anything that happened between me and your mother. And don't you talk to me in that tone."

Stiles basically ignored his father's words. "Oh, that's where you're wrong. You do owe me an explanation. My mother may be gone to glory, but there's a child out there, a brother or sister I have somewhere. One that is from what she says in these letters, is the product of rape." Stiles patted the top of the red box and then walked closer to Pastor and gave the box to him. "Now, tell me why you forced her to keep a child that wasn't even yours and one that was by some sick, evil minded excuse of a human being? Why did you do that to her?" Stiles anger increased.

Pastor bowed his head and slowly opened the red box. "Two wrongs don't make a right. And Audrey and I, well we wanted children of our own. Not that I didn't love you as my son, but she wanted to give me a child so bad, but it just didn't happen, but it just never happened for us.

I was at the church the night she was raped. We had finished Bible study but I had a meeting with the ministers at the church so your mother decided she was going to leave, run by Wal-Mart and then head home and wait on me. Only she was raped behind where that Wal-Mart on American Way used to be." Pastor's head still hung low, averting Stiles' piercing gaze.

"Why don't I remember any of this?" Stiles asked, shaking his head and biting his lower lip.

"Because, Son, you were just a kid, only about five years old, and we made sure we kept it from you. That woman was a true warrior. She survived. Praise God."

"You sit here talking about 'oh, your mother was a true warrior. Praise God.' Well, I don't want to hear that crap. You forced my mother," Stiles balled his hands into fists and pounded his chest with his right hand. "to have another man's child. A man who tried to kill her? What kind of person are you?" Stiles looked sickened by what he was hearing from Pastor. "And why didn't they give her that, that pill? That morning after pill so she wouldn't get pregnant? Did you stop them from doing that too?"

Pastor's face transformed into a mask of rage. He lashed out as he stared up toward Stiles. "Of course I didn't stop the doctors from doing all they could to help your mother. And not that it's any of your business, but they did give her the pill, but she still ended up being pregnant. Plus, it wasn't until a few weeks later, when it was time for her period and she missed it, that we really got nervous. At first we thought the stress and trauma of being sexually assaulted kept her from having a cycle. But the following month came and she still hadn't come on her period so she went to see an ob/gyn. They ran a pregnancy test, and the rest is history.

I didn't want her to have an abortion because it was a high probability that the child she was carrying could be mine. But after Francesca was born, we did a DNA test and...."

"Francesca? Francesca is not your biological daughter?" Stiles took a step backward like he was about to fall, but he managed to steady himself. "No wonder mother acted like she did toward her. And you, you did nothing about it."

"She *is* my daughter. I don't care what some DNA test says. I loved Francesca from the time she was in your mother's womb up until this very day. So don't you stand there like some pompous, self-righteous idiot," Pastor yelled. "I wouldn't change one thing if it meant Francesca wasn't in my life. God works in mysterious ways."

"Don't blame this on God. What you did to Audrey was dead wrong. You weren't the one who was raped and tortured. You weren't the one who had to feel a baby growing inside her belly for nine months while knowing that the man who impregnated her wasn't you but a monster. And you say you loved my mother? You were thinking about yourself, and probably doubting your own manhood," Stiles continued to yell and rant.

Pastor wobbled but stood to his feet. "Get out. I will not allow you to point a finger at me. You have no idea what me and your mother went through. What you read, her letters to me, was personal. It wasn't for you. You crossed the line, son. And I'm disappointed in you." Pastor's voice quivered.

Stiles laughed nervously. "You call me self-righteous. If I am, then obviously I got it from you. All this time, my sister has lived knowing that she had a mother who practically hated her guts. And she never understood why. All the time you had the answers and you refused to tell her or me, not even after our mother died. I guess you were protecting yourself. At the expense of my mother, you made her have a baby to cover your own butt."

Pastor yelled louder and pointed toward Stiles. "I said, leave. When you're ready to sit down and talk to me like a man then you need to go."

"I never thought I'd see a day like today. A day when the respect I had for a man I called father is gone. I despise you."

Stiles turned abruptly and within a few steps he had opened the front door and bolted outside. Tears blinded his sight as he walked to his car, got inside and sped off.

"Francesca, Francesca," he said through his tears. "Mother, mother why did you listen to him? Why, oh God help me through this."

12

"The heart is the only broken instrument that works." T.E. Kalem

Rena rushed over to the trash can and chunked the box of condoms inside with as much force as she could muster. "I am so freaking mad," she screamed. "How could Stiles be so cruel and vicious? How could he tell his wife about me?"

She opened the door to her bedroom and ran up the hall to the guest room. "Delores, I can't go through with it," she screamed.

Delores bolted upright in the bed like she'd been poked with a branding iron. "What? What are you talking about?" she asked, her voice groggy from having just woke up.

"I'm telling you that I can't marry him."

Delores rubbed her eyes as she got up and out of the bed. "Are you on drugs or something? Of course, you can marry him, and you are going to marry him. This is your wedding day. Those nervous jitters will pass as soon as you see your man standing next to you."

Rena placed both hands over her ears. "Noooo, don't you see," she yelled. "How can I marry him after what Stiles and Detria have done?"

"So, it was Stiles who sent those condoms? And Detria? Isn't that his wife?"

"Yes, that's his wife. And the card was addressed from both of them. It was just a cruel thing to do."

Delores walked over and stood next to her sister. "Look, it wasn't the brightest thing to do, that I admit, but it's certainly not enough to make you call off a wedding. Maybe it was a sick, stupid prank. Stiles, from what mamma says, still loves you. Sometimes people do stupid things all in the name of love. Maybe he sent those condoms because he doesn't want you getting pregnant by anyone if it isn't him. I know that sounds crazy, but it's not impossible, you know." Delores wrapped an arm around Rena to console her.

"If only you knew."

"I don't know, so tell me. I have no idea why you and Stiles broke up. I don't know why you moved back to Andover. All I know is what you and mama told me, which was you and Stiles tried but just couldn't make your marriage work."

"I wish I could tell you everything, but I just can't. And now I can't marry Robert. He's already gone through a lot with me, and I won't take a chance of Stiles or his so called bride doing anything else to try to ruin this. I'd rather Robert be hurt now than for my past to be thrown up in my face over and over again. He doesn't deserve that."

"Robert loves you, Rena. I don't know much about him either, but I do know that when that man looks at you, all I see is love, unconditional love. Stop giving Stiles and his wife power over your life. You're better than that, Rena. And maybe something really, really bad caused your marriage to him to crumble, but that's all in the past. Don't let Stiles keep beating you over the head with this foolishness. He's no longer a part of your life. Your new life starts in a few hours. And I have a feeling it's going to be fabulous."

Rena looked at Delores. "I'm going to call him."

"Call who? Robert? No, please don't do that, Rena. Don't mess this up," Delores pleaded.

"I'm not talking about Robert. I'm going to call Stiles. I need to know why he would do me like this." Rena ran out of the room and went into the living room where she retrieved her cell phone off the sofa table. She began to scroll through her phone until she saw Stiles' cell phone number. She'd put it under a fake name just in case Robert ever had a notion to go through her phone.

"Don't do that. Don't call him," Delores ordered as she walked up behind Rena. "That's what he wants you to do. He wants to see you miserable. Don't give him the pleasure, Rena. Please."

Rena pushed the button and the phone started ringing. "I have to do this for me and for Robert. Stiles has to know that he needs to stay out of my life. Him and his wife."

The phone rang several times before it rolled over to Stiles' voicemail. Rena listened. "You've reached Pastor Stiles Graham. Your call is important to me, so please leave a message and I will return your call at my earliest convenience. Remember that God loves you and there's nothing you can do about it."

"Stiles, it's Rena. I got your little gift, and I want to let you know that I don't appreciate your constant interference in my life. If you don't leave me alone, you will be sorry. I'll do whatever I have to do to keep you away from me. Even if it means coming to your church and putting you on blast for stalking me." Rena's tone was venomous. It was her wedding day, but she couldn't enjoy it thanks to Stiles Graham.

"Okay, so you called and left him a message. Now go on and get your clothes on. You have to get to the beauty salon and after that we have to get to the church. You have a wedding to attend." Delores smiled at Rena who remained somber looking.

"I still don't know whether I should go through with this wedding. I just don't feel right. I feel like this is a sign, an ominous sign too."

Delores followed Rena into her galley style kitchen. "Don't let Stiles or his wife, or anybody for that matter, ruin your day and control your life. If anything, if you're so disturbed by what he did, then talk to somebody in law enforcement. You may be able to file a complaint against him, perhaps for stalking, but do not, and I mean do not let him have you all bent out of shape. You deserve to be happy; and I believe Robert makes you happy."

Rena stood next to the refrigerator and exhaled. "I know you're right. But I still feel out of sorts about marrying him. I mean , I do love him, but well, it's just a different feeling from when I married Stiles. Back then I was so excited that I could hardly contain myself. And with Robert I was ready to call this whole thing off. I mean with Stiles doing what he did, sending me that horrible so-called gift. It reminds me too much of my past."

Rena couldn't tear her thoughts away from Stiles and what he'd done. As much as she tried to focus on her wedding, it was virtually impossible.

"Like I told you, forget about him and anyone connected with him for that matter, including his wife, his sister, his daddy. All of them. Believe me, you'll feel better once you're Mrs. Robert Becton. You'll see," Delores said.

"I hope you're right. I really do, because the last thing I want to do is hurt him."

◊

Delores escorted Rena into the side entrance of the church. Meryl rushed over to both of her daughters as soon as they stepped foot inside.

"Come on, Rena, let's go to the fellowship hall. The caterer is in there making sure everything is set. I want you to see for yourself, then we'll go to the dressing room and start getting ready."

"Hi, to you too, Mama," Rena responded, then turned and smiled at Delores.

"That's our mother," Delores added.

"What on earth are you two talking about? What did I do?"

Delores waved her hand. "Oh, nothing, Ma. Come on, let's go check out the caterer again."

Rena slowly trailed along next to her mother and sister. Delores didn't understand her dilemma. Robert had already accepted her past when it was thrown up in his face by Frankie. Rena still thought from time to time about how Frankie told Robert about their affair. And she told him at First Lady Audrey's repast – how foul was that.

Frankie was a piece of work. She had it in for Rena at one time, but right after that incident, Frankie asked Rena to forgive her for ruining her life. Rena said that she would, but there were times like these when she couldn't stand anyone in the Graham family.

Stiles wanted folks to believe that he was all holier than thou when, in Rena's eyes, he was an unforgiving, vindictive, revenge seeking man. So why couldn't she hate him? Why did she let him get her so worked up, mess with her mind the way he did?

"What do you think? I think he's done a great job with the menu. Everything looks and smells good. And on top of that, the room is nicely decorated," said Meryl. "What do you think, sweetie?" She asked Rena.

"I like it," she said half-heartedly. Rena's mind was not on how good the food looked or tasted, or how pretty the reception hall was decorated, she was having second thoughts about walking down the aisle. *wedding jitters,* she thought.

"Where is your mind? You act like you're somewhere else," Delores said to Rena.

"I said I like it." Rena turned and walked toward the exit. "I'm satisfied with the way everything looks, so let's go to the dressing room," Rena insisted.

"Ooookay," her mother said.

The three ladies ran into Robert's sister as they rounded the hall leading to the dressing room. The four of them chatted while they started getting dressed.

"Rena, how long are you going to be off work?" his sister asked.

"I took Thursday and Friday off so me and Robert will have a long weekend. Robert did the same, and we'll go back to work Monday."

"No honeymoon, huh?" Delores said.

“We’re going on sort of a honeymoon this weekend,” Rena said and managed to smile. “We both agreed that we’d do the real honeymoon thing on our first wedding anniversary. You know we just closed on our new house a few weeks ago. I want to decorate it and that takes money, so we decided to forego a honeymoon for now. So in lieu of that, we’re spending the weekend at the Four Seasons, the one that’s in downtown Boston.”

“Umm,” her mother said. “You and Robert are going to do it up. That’s a five star hotel.” Meryl sounded impressed. “Sounds like a honeymoon to me.” She quipped.

“I hope the two of you are happy for many years to come,” said Delores.

Rena inhaled and slowly released it, closing her eyes for a second as she thought about the gorgeous river views the hotel offered. Talking about the honeymoon quickly made her forget what Stiles had done.

◊

“Are you ready?” her father asked as he extended his elbow out for her to loop her arms in his.

Rena looked at her dad, and smiled as she stood behind the doors leading into the sanctuary. “I guess I’m as ready as I’m ever going to be,” Rena responded. She looked radiant in an off white, chiffon, halter, A-line gown that had a flowing side drape. The gown reflected Rena’s natural beauty to perfection.

As Rena glided along the aisle, her mind cleared of all outside interference, and finally she was able to see the man waiting on her at the altar. Robert looked handsome. His eyes connected with Rena’s and she saw his lips turn upward and form a tooth-showing smile.

Rena returned his smile with a warm smile of her own. She felt like he was a magnet and she was a piece of copper or iron being pulled toward him. How could she keep on doubting that this was where she was supposed to be? This man was the man she was supposed to be with. It was time for her to let go of her past. It was time to walk in her new life without clinging to her past life.

◊

Rena giggled in Robert's arms as he carried her across the threshold of the deluxe garden hotel suite that could easily pass for a studio apartment. The king bed, large bathroom, spacious sitting area with bay window and a spectacular view of the Public Garden and Boston Common rendered Rena speechless.

Robert kicked the door closed with the heel of his foot. Rena allowed herself to be indulged by her new husband. Upon entering their hotel suite, she was met with a trail of red roses leading from the doorway to the bedroom. A bottle of champagne was chilling in an ice bucket, and sensual music played softly in the background.

Robert carried her to the bed and eased her down.. Trying to control his physical excitement, he slowly positioned himself on top of her. Instantly the caress of his lips on her mouth and along her body set her aflame. Parting her lips, she raised herself up to meet him. His hands tugged at her wedding dress, and found their way underneath the gown and up to her intimate places.

Rena responded by pushing lightly against him and with Robert's help, she removed her wedding gown and he quickly got out of his tux. He eased the cup of her bra aside and his hands moved magically over her small mountains. Aroused she surrendered completely and gasped when he made her all his. She was drawn into a passion that she'd never known before.

Rena lay in the curve of Robert's arms. She had never felt this way with Stiles. She never had the chance because of her STD and the fact that she hid it from him by withholding sex from Stiles. At the time, it was the only way Rena could protect him. He didn't know that Francesca had infected her and it was too late for their marriage after he found out.

"I love you. You know that?" he whispered in her ear.

"I love you too, baby. I love you so much." She sighed in pleasant exhaustion.

13

"Fear not for the future, weep not for the past." Percy Bysshe

Francesca looked at the caller ID on her cell phone. It was Stiles. "What could he want?" Francesca and her family had basically reconciled and set aside their differences, but she still didn't talk to them that often, especially now since she was Tim's wife. Tim's family embraced her, AIDS and all. It was what Francesca loved about them and Tim. Tim's family didn't seem the least bit fazed about her AIDS. For that reason alone, Francesca considered them to be her family. She was loved and accepted just the way she was, with all of her imperfections, with all of the baggage she came into Tim's life carrying. But she felt loved for the first time in her life and Tim's love felt good, really good.

"Hello," Francesca answered.

"Hi, sis," Stiles said in a rather odd, yet gentle tone. "What's going on?"

"Living, taking it one day at a time. You?" she asked.

"We need to talk," he said.

"Talk then," countered Francesca.

"In person. As soon as possible," Stiles told her.

"Uh, uh. I know what that means. Drama, drama and more drama. And there's no more drama for me, Stiles. I'm living my life, not bothering you, or Pastor. I'm trying to take care of me for once. It's not like I have a lot of time left on this earth. And it's not because of the Mayan Calendar and 2012 either," she remarked with light bitterness.

"This is important. It's something I think you'd want to know. It'll explain why Audrey treated you the way she did all those years," he explained.

"I already know the answer to that. She hated me. Plain and simple. The woman had no love at all for her one and only daughter. Whatever excuse you want to make for her, well, that's on you, but I don't want to hear it, Stiles," she said firmly.

"Francesca, you're going to want to hear this. Believe me. I'm driving up there first thing Monday morning."

"Look, you can't tell me what you're about to do when it comes to seeing me. I see you on my own time, when I say so."

"Okay, I'm sorry about that. May I come to see you Monday? Is that better?" he asked.

Francesca was silent.

"You there?" Stiles asked.

"Yeah, you can come, but make it before noon. Me and Tim have plans for later that afternoon. So, if you can't come then, too bad."

"I'll be there. And Francesca, I think Tim needs to be there with you. What I have to tell you might knock you off your feet."

"I don't think whatever it is can make me feel any differently than I do about Audrey already. The woman gave birth to me, but that's about all she did. I guess I should be grateful for that, but anything else...when it comes to her, I'm good. She's made her mark on my life and I don't want to be drawn back into her mess."

"This is no mess. I'm going to share some truth with you, Francesca. That's all."

"We'll talk about it when you come. I gotta go."

"Sure, sis. I'll see you Monday. Bye."

"Bye."

"What was that all about?" Tim asked.

"That was my brother. He says he knows why my mother treated me the way she did while I was growing up. He wants to come up here Monday to tell me about it."

"You sure you want to do that?" His voice hardened. "I mean, you've gone through a lot in your life already. I don't see how bringing up something that happened in the past will help you feel better."

Francesca released a long, audible breath. "I know, but by the same token, whatever he has to tell me, I'd rather he go on and tell me now. If not, knowing Stiles he'll call and call until I give in. He's always tried to justify Audrey's actions and I guess it doesn't make a difference that she's dead." Francesca shrugged her shoulders.

"Okay, it's your call." He leaned in next to her and kissed her, followed by a light chuckle.

"What's so funny?"

"Oh, nothing. It's just being with you, having you as my wife, makes me happy. I love you, Francesca."

Francesca looked deeply into his sexy eyes. "I love you too. I don't know what I would do without you, Tim. You, I mean you loved me when I was at my lowest, when I wasn't loveable. You are a God sent man, and I want to live out the rest of my days with you." She massaged the side of his face with the back of her hand.

Francesca still couldn't believe the deep feelings that had evolved toward Brother Tim. Initially, when he confessed his feelings to her she thought something was wrong with him. That maybe he was well, *slow*, is what she called him. But it didn't take long, not long at all for Francesca to realize that Tim was a real, true-life man of God. He had the gift of looking past a person's appearance and seeing the kind of person they were on the inside. He took people at face value. Something Francesca believed she did as well, only it had backfired on her in a terrible, terrible way.

Growing up, falling in love, and getting married was something Francesca had rarely thought about. When Fonda started molesting her, Francesca thought about it then. Thinking of being with a boy and falling in love helped her to remember that what Fonda made her do was wrong. But her brief, childlike thought of boys was forever damaged when Pastor Travis, the former youth minister of Holy Rock, raped her right in his office at Holy Rock. She refused to trust anybody anymore.

It was the main reason Francesca turned away from God. She thought if God was supposed to love her so much, then why did he let Fonda and Minister Travis do those things to her? God had to hate her, is what she came to believe. Francesca grew angrier toward Him the more she relived her molestation and rape. She credited her friendship with Rena for helping her to survive.

Francesca felt a kindred spirit with Rena. They were both fifteen years old when their friendship changed into a sexual relationship. They had been old enough to understand the decision they made, but too young to believe it mattered.

Francesca believed Rena and her to be best friends, but she still could never tell Rena about what had happened to her; she was too ashamed and embarrassed to tell anyone, including the police.

As their friendship strengthened, and shortly after Minister Travis raped her, Francesca vowed she would never under any circumstances, let another man touch her. Then she thought about Fonda and told herself to choose the lesser of two evils. *Fonda,* Francesca had decided. *I can be in control with another woman. I can be like Fonda. That way no one, male or female, can ever hurt me like that again,* she'd thought all those years ago.

"You make me feel," Francesca broke out singing and grinning at the same time. *"Uuuuuu make me feel."*

Tim leaned backward on the sofa and started laughing at his wife.

"I said, uuuuuuuu make me feel like a nat...u...ral...woman." Francesca's cat, Jabez, started meowing and strolled away from where he was propped against her ankles.

"You are so bad, so bad." His fingers curling underneath her chin as he spoke. Next he kissed the crown of her hairless head. "And I love every note of it."

Francesca popped her head up and started chuckling this time. "You are so full of it, Brother Tim

Swift. You'll use anything to try to seduce me, won't you?" she asked him between laughing.

"You can't blame a man for trying." He lifted both hands and hunched his shoulders.

Playfully, Francesca hit him on his shoulder. "At least I was singing the truth, or trying to sing the truth. 'Cause you do make me feel like a woman. I can't ever remember feeling like a real woman, a natural woman. You know what, Tim?"

"No, I don't know what. So tell me," he answered as he tenderly toyed with her right ear.

"I think I can honestly say that I've missed feeling this feeling that I feel when I'm with you. God never gave up on me. He brought me back around. Gave me another chance to live, to experience genuine love from him and love from him through you. I'm a woman, Tim. I'm a real woman."

Francesca looked at herself like she was unfamiliar with her own skin. Perhaps in a way she was because she saw herself differently. Francesca had come to love herself. She'd finally started the process of forgiving herself knowing that God already had.

"You are a real woman, Francesca. And that's why I fell in love with you so easily. You were wounded, but we all are in some way. I know I am," Tim emphasized. "I'm just grateful that God loved me so much that He blessed me with you," Tim said then stood up from the couch. He reached his hand toward Francesca. She accepted it and stood up.

He nipped her on the lip. "Now, what do you want to eat today, natural woman? Do you feel like going out?"

Her smiled widened. "I believe I do feel like going out. It's a beautiful day outside, it's not too humid, and plus I've been feeling pretty since we've been back home. Those herbs and my changed diet are really doing wonders on this body. Thank God for that."

"Great." Tim rubbed his hands together. "So where would my natural woman like to go?"

"I have a taste for one of those vegetable shish kabobs from that new place in midtown." Francesca licked her lips.

"ALL Veggies?"

"Yeah, that's it."

"Okay, ALL Veggies it is. Let's get out of here."

"I'm ready," she answered. She grabbed hold of the cane parked next to her and stood up.

Tim took hold of her free hand, and the two of them left their house to go enjoy spending time with one another over a good meal.

◊

"So what do you think your brother has to tell you?" Tim asked as he poked a pile of nachos 'n cheese on his fork and guided it into his mouth.

"I don't know, and honestly I don't care. Do you think it's wrong for me to feel like that?"

"Baby, from all you've told me, you've been through a lot with your family, especially your mother, so I understand the reason you feel the way you do. But on the other hand, you know I'm going to tell you how I feel from a Godly standpoint."

Francesca picked up her glass of lemon water, took a sip and nodded her head. "Yea, I know. So let it rip."

"You already know one of my favorite passages in the Bible talks about letting go of the past. Right?"

"Right," Francesca answered while pulling a piece of red bell pepper off the kabob and popping it into her mouth. "And I'm trying to let go of the past. Believe me, Tim. But it's hard. Every time I think about my life and all of the horrible things that were done to me and the terrible things I did to myself, I get all messed up on the inside. I've made so many mistakes and to add insult to injury, my own mother acted like she despised me." Tears gathered up in the corners of her eyes. Francesca wiped them away before they had a chance to fall down her face.

Tim extended his hand and used his thumb to brush away the remaining tears. "It's going to be just fine. You'll see. But first you have to stop looking back, Francesca. You have to forget what's behind you, baby, and strain toward what's ahead. And what is remembering the past going to do but keep you bound and upset? You know what the Bible teaches us about that."

Francesca frowned, put down her fork and exchanged it for her glass of water. "I know, but still, it's easy for you to say. You had a normal childhood with two loving parents and two sisters who still spoil you to this day. You have no idea what it's like to be an outcast, to be raised in a household that's supposed to be so spiritual but nothing but hell going on in the inside. Here my father was, a preacher, a pastor of a church, standing up Sunday after Sunday preaching the word of God. But his own house was falling apart. And my mother, let's not even go there with her. She was parading all up in Holy Rock, dressed to the nines and acting like she was all that, when she was nothing but evil and lowdown. All she cared about was what other folks thought."

"Look." Tim reached out and grabbed Francesca's trembling hands and wrapped them inside his. "We're not going to do this. We're supposed to be having a good time this evening, not rehashing all the hurt of yesterday or comparing each other's pasts. Okay?" he said then caressed her cheek.

Francesca stared into his inviting sea green eyes. "You're right. It just gets so hard sometimes. And now Stiles is coming up here with more drama from my past. Tim, I just don't know how much more of this I can take. Why couldn't I have had a normal childhood, with a normal family like yours? Why did it have to be me?"

Tim placed two fingers on her lips. "Shhh, stop that. You're not going to go back to questioning why things happened the way they did. The important thing is that you're here, right now, with me and you are loved. I love you more than life itself, Francesca. My family is crazy about you. Our church family loves you, but most importantly, God loves you. And if you don't want to see Stiles or hear what he has to say, then don't see him. It's simple as that. You're one tough cookie and you know as good as I do that if you tell him that you don't want to hear whatever it is he wants to tell you, then he can't do anything but respect that."

"I know. You're right, but I'm going to let him come on up here and get it over with. Then I'm going to tell him that whatever else he has to say, he needs to tell it to somebody else because I'm not hearing it."

"See, that's my girl." Tim smiled and so did Francesca. "Now let's finish grubbing before our food gets cold."

"I love you, Tim."

"Of course you do. How can you not love a good-looking, suave fellow like myself," he said jokingly.

"Boy, please. Eat your food so nothing else crazy comes out of your mouth," Francesca responded.

They laughed together and Francesca pushed the worries of the past out of her mind, and concentrated on the man sitting across the table.

14

"Simply having children does not make mothers." John A. Shedd

Stiles pulled up in the driveway, opened the door to the garage of his home and much to his surprise his wife's car was parked in her space. "She better be here," he mumbled. "I've had too much to deal with today and her shenanigans is something I'm not going to put up with."

He parked next to her, got out of his vehicle and slammed the door, and walked toward the entrance into their spacious home.

"I'm home, " he shouted. No response "I'm home," he said again as he walked from the kitchen into the hallway. Still nothing. He made his way up the stairs and into the master bedroom. Laying across the bed was Detria minus Baby Audrey. He stared at her for several seconds before he turned and walked down the hall to the nursery. No Baby Audrey.

Where in the world is my daughter? Lord, help me to keep my calm. He bolted back to the bedroom.

"Where is Audrey?" he yelled as soon as he darted the door of their bedroom.

Detria jumped up suddenly. "What?" she asked like she was confused. "Why are you yelling?"

"I said, where is my daughter?"

"Oh, she's with Mother Brown," Detria answered nonchalantly. She got up and slowly walked toward their on-suite master bathroom.

"Oh, no you don't," Stiles said and with two giant steps he was at her side and holding her by the elbow.

"Take your hands off me," Detria yelled. "Don't even think about—"

"Don't think about what?" Stiles barked. "Tell me why she's with Mother Brown and not with her own mother, Detria?" He loosened his grip on her but he bit into his lower lip.

"I've been at the church practically all day with your daughter," she said like she was mad. "I have to tend to her while you run off to church or to that university. You have all the time you want to run around but as soon as I leave her for a few hours with someone we both trust," she said with emphasis, "you want to come up in here yelling and flying all off the handle. Now, I told you, she's with Mother Brown. She's going to bring her to church tomorrow. That way I can get me some rest tonight and get up early tomorrow morning, go to church and get things set up for our first Children's church service in the new Children's Center."

"You're telling me she's supposed to spend the night away from home? Are you crazy?" Stiles fumed. He was furious. How could Detria leave their child for somebody else to take care of. True enough, Mother Brown was someone he trusted to take care of his daughter, but only when they really needed her services. And being tired was not a good enough reason for Stiles. What kind of first time mother would dare think about leaving their baby with someone else? Was Detria gone mad or what?

"Call Mother Brown," he ordered and picked up their landline phone from the night stand and shoved it toward Detria.

Detria looked at the cordless phone in Stiles' hand and attempted to walk past him. "I'm not calling her. For what? Audrey is fine. She's probably down for the night anyway."

"I said, call her and tell her you're on your way to get our child."

Detria stopped, put her hands on her hip and said, "And I said, I'm not doing it. If you want her, you go get her and you're going to stay up with her all night if you bring her home. You know for yourself if you wake her up from her sleep, she's going to be up all night long. She's just like your mother, cranky," Detria smarted off and dashed past Stiles and into their bathroom, pushing the door closed behind her.

Stiles balled up his fist and hit the door so hard it put a hole in it.

Detria opened it up. "What in the world is wrong with you? Are you gone mad or something? Look at my door," she continued ranting. "You're going to fix it, Stiles. I don't know what your problem is lately with all of these violent outbursts, but you've got the wrong sister. I'm not going to sit back and let you beat on me. You think you miss your precious little Audrey now, wait until I up and leave your tail. Keep on acting like you all big and bad," she pointed a lone finger at him, "and you're going to find yourself up in this house all alone, Mr. Preacher Boy cause me and your daughter will be outta here. Believe that," she said and turned away and went back into the bathroom.

Stiles found it hard to believe that she had threatened to leave him and take his daughter with her. He rubbed his hand over his head and started pacing across the span of the spacious bedroom. His cell phone rang from the clip on his belt.

He ignored it. The phone rang again. He ignored it. It rang again. This time Stiles removed it from the clip, glanced at the ID and then answered it.

"What is it, Pastor?" Stiles said as soon as he pushed the green TALK button. "I don't want to hear any more of your excuses. I don't want to hear an apology for screwing up not only my mother's life but my sister's as well."

The door to the bathroom opened and Detria slowly walked out, arms folded. She stood almost directly in front of Stiles.

"I said I don't want to hear it," he screamed. "And you call yourself a man of God. How could you force my mother to keep a child that you know was the result of a rape?"

Detria's hand flew up to her mouth. "What?" she screamed. "Who are you talking about? Audrey, your mother? Who? Frankie, I mean Francesca?"

Stiles turned and walked out of the room and went to his study. This time it was his turn to slam the door in Detria's face, and he did just that, locking it as well. In between his father's pleas for understanding and forgiveness, he heard the doorknob being turned back and forth followed by Detria pounding on the door.

"Let me in," she yelled from the other side. "I have a right to know what's going on in this family, Stiles Graham. Open this door," she screamed.

Stiles ignored her and remained focused on telling Pastor exactly how he felt. "I don't care if you believe in abortion or not. It was not your decision and you had no right to impose your beliefs down my mother's throat."

"Son, listen. I know what your mother said in that letter, but honest it's not like you think."

"You're a liar, and you know it and God knows it. And to think all of my life I've thought of you as my father. But you're nothing but a bully. You used God's word against my mother. You twisted it and made her feel like she would be wrong if she aborted the seed of a rapist."

"When your mother said she was pregnant, it was hard, extremely hard for both of us. You think that I didn't feel sickened by what had happened. If only I had been there that night then I could have stopped it, but I wasn't. But God is still in control, even though what happened was horrific."

"It was more than horrific. I'm sure it was devastating for her. To have someone violate you like that."

"But still, the fact remains, having an abortion was not the answer. And just think about it; if you'll do that you'll agree with me. You wouldn't have your sister if Audrey had aborted her, and I wouldn't have been blessed with my dear, darling Francesca."

"Open the door," Detria kept yelling.

Stiles clinched his mouth and chuckled nastily, all while ignoring Detria. "Are you serious? Blessed? Do you think Francesca is going to feel that way when she finds out the truth? And what about her life and the way mother treated her? How is that a blessing? Sounds more like a curse to me. My sister has been going through pure hell since the time she was a little girl. And she's never known why. All the time you had the answers. All the time it was because of a decision you made over my mother's life? No wonder you acted like a spineless man when it came to Audrey."

Pastor's voice escalated over the phone. "Don't you call me spineless. I did what I thought was best. I prayed about it and God gave me a peace about it. He wanted us to have Francesca. I know He did," Pastor said vehemently. "Me and your mother talked a long time about whether she should keep the baby or not. It wasn't me who forced her to have that child; we both agreed on it."

"You forget her true feelings are in black and white, Pastor. She said in that letter that you forced her to keep that baby. And I believe her. I believe every word she said. I used to think she was the controlling one, but all the time it's been you. You ran up to Holy Rock day in and day out, leaving my mother here to get raped and then forcing her to keep the baby. I don't know what it was, or maybe you couldn't give her a baby so you wanted everyone to believe Francesca was yours."

"Stop it, stop it right now. It wasn't that I couldn't have children. That's not true at all. Your mother just never got pregnant again. Doctors called it unexplained infertility. In other words, there was no reason she shouldn't have been able to get pregnant after Francesca, but she didn't. And as year after year passed and she didn't get pregnant, we both believed even stronger that it had been God's will for your mother to have Francesca."

"Too bad my mother can't tell her side of the story. Oh, but she can and she did. In that letter. That letter says it all. So I don't want to hear anything you have to say. I'm telling Francesca about you and your hypocrisy. We'll see what she thinks about you then," Stiles said, his voice cold and accusing.

"Don't do that to your sister," Pastor said, his voice sounding defeated. "This will tear her apart, and she's already ill. Why would you want to tell her—"

"Hold up, don't try to make me feel guilty for something you're to blame for. My sister deserves to know what kind of man you are. Standing behind the Word to make yourself look all holier than thou. I've had enough of you." Stiles abruptly pushed the END button on his iPhone.

He walked over to the door and opened it. Detria was gone. *Good, she better be gone to get my daughter.*

◊

Detria sped off up the street and out of the confines of their upscale neighborhood. She voice dialed Pastor's number for the third time since getting inside her car. The first two times, Pastor didn't answer. Detria knew it was because he was still talking to Stiles, but she refused to give up. She had to know what was going on and what Stiles meant when he said Pastor forced Audrey to have a baby. Could it be true? Had Pastor done something so despicable? The third time is a charm is what some folks say, and it worked for Detria because Pastor picked up the third time around.

"Hello," he answered.

"Pastor, it's Detria. Are you all right?" she asked, feigning concern.

"No, how can I be all right. Feels like my whole world is collapsing." He sounded like he was crying.

"I'm on my way over there. I should be there in about twenty minutes."

"No, don't do that. I need some time alone with God. I need to pray about this."

"I'm coming over there," Detria insisted. "I promise I won't stay long, but I need to make sure you're all right. I'll see you shortly," she said before she ended the call and accelerated her speed as she jumped on I-240.

Detria voice dialed the next number. A male answered.

"What's up?" he asked.

"You home yet?" she replied.

"Naw. I should be there in about an hour. Why? You coming to see me or something?" he said and snickered into the phone.

"Maybe. So much has happened since I saw you this afternoon. My husband acted like he wanted to get violent again with me because I left the baby with Mother Brown tonight. And you know I've been working my tail off trying to get things in perfect order for tomorrow. I lug that baby around with me everywhere I go and he wants to trip because I leave her for one night so I can make him look good tomorrow? Please, that man is getting on my nerves. I'm about ready to call it a wrap with this marriage."

"Naw, hold up. Calm your feisty little butt down," the man said into the phone. "Where are you? Hiding in the bathroom somewhere?"

"No, actually I'm on my way to Pastor's house."

"To Pastor's house? For what? Counseling? If that's what you need, baby I'll give you all the counseling you need and then some," he told her.

"I'm serious, Skip. Every day I'm finding out more and more that the Graham family is nothing but a bunch of phonies."

"Look, I'm trying to maneuver myself out of this parking garage. It's swarming with folks leaving this game. How long are you going to be at his house?" Skip asked.

"Long enough to find out what Stiles refused to tell me."

"What do you mean by long enough to find out what my boy refused to tell you?"

"All I know is there's something about Audrey and Francesca. I think she's the child of a rapist."

"Who? Francesca?"

"Yes, Francesca," Detria responded.

"Hey, I tell you what, hit me up when you leave the pastor's house."

"Okay. I'll talk to you in a minute. Bye, babe."

"Yea, later," Skip answered.

◊

Stiles searched every room of their house. Detria was not there. *She certainly isn't up in here sneaking on the phone talking to whoever. Let me check this garage.*

When Stiles saw Detria's car was gone, a sense of welcome relief came over him. *She's gone to get my daughter.* Convinced that she was headed to Mother Brown's to pick up Baby Audrey, Stiles returned upstairs, took a bath and went to his study to go over his message for tomorrow's three services.

"One bad apple," he spoke out loud and paced along the cherry hardwood floors of his study. "One bad apple won't spoil the whole bunch. That's what some people believe. But I want you to know today that you can't believe what everybody throws your way. You see, one bad apple can spoil the whole bunch. David says in Psalm one and one 'Blessed is the man that walketh not in the counsel of the ungodly, nor standeth in the way of sinners, nor sitteth in the seat of the scornful.' If one sinner can't tarnish you, then why does the Psalm say otherwise? Why does the Psalmist say you're blessed when you don't follow the counsel of the ungodly. Why shouldn't you stand in the midst of sinners or sit at their table. It's because you will find yourself like the Psalmist; first simply walking along with the ungodly, then you get a little more comfortable and so you start standing or hanging around with people you know are up to no good, then before you realize it you're sitting down with the very people who can get you into a world of mess. It happens every day. Look at all the people in jail who are guilty by association. I tell you," Stiles preached to himself, "one bad apple can spoil the whole bunch..."

After spending an hour going over his sermon, Stiles stopped and looked at his watch. It was going on ten o'clock at night and Detria hadn't returned with Baby Audrey. He retrieved his cell phone, scrolled through his contacts until he located Mother Brown's number. He walked over to the landline phone on his desk and called her.

Mother Brown answered, her voice sounding heavy with sleep. "Mother Brown, I'm sorry to disturb you, but—"

"Look, Pastor Graham, I told First Lady before she left little Audrey over here for the night to be sure y'all wouldn't be over there worrying. That precious child hasn't been an ounce of trouble. She's in there in my grandson's room in his bed fast asleep. She had a time playing with him. After I fed her dinner and gave her a good warm bath, she fell right to sleep. I did him the same way and he went to sleep too, so you and the First Lady get you some rest. Tomorrow is going to be a long day. I'm really excited that the Children's Center is going to be opening tomorrow. I know you are too, aren't you Pastor Graham?"

"Mother Brown did you say Baby Audrey is asleep?"

"Yes, I sure did. What did you expect?"

"Uh, when was the last time you spoke with First Lady?" Stiles asked.

"Earlier this afternoon. Is everything all right?" Mother Brown asked.

"Oh, yes, yes ma'am. Maybe I should come and get the baby," Stiles said, not understanding what games Detria was playing with him.

"No, you are not coming over here and waking her up out of her sleep, and I'm not getting up out of my bed to let you in just so you can have this precious little one up all night because you missed her. I'm telling you, she's fine, Pastor Graham. Now, please you and the First Lady get some sleep. Me and Brother Brown will bring Audrey to church. So see y'all in the morning, if God says the same. Goodnight now, Pastor."

"Yes, Mother Brown. Thank you so much and God bless you and Brother Brown."

"Thank you, Pastor."

After the call ended Stiles grew angry all over again. "Detria, where the world are you?"

15

"An eye for an eye makes the whole world blind."
Mahatma Gandhi

"Pastor, are you saying that you told First Lady Audrey that she should keep a baby after what happened to her? And," added Detria, knowing that the child she was carrying could very well be his child and not yours? Is that what you're telling me?" Detria inquired hungrily.

Pastor appeared quiet, withdrawn and worried as he sat in his recliner listening to Detria grill him about his past. He couldn't believe that Stiles would share such intimate information about their family with Detria. He didn't care if Detria was Stiles' wife; in Pastor's opinion she still had no right to be privy to his and Audrey's personal business. Frankly, he was sickened by the whole thing. If Stiles hadn't been so nosy, none of this would have occurred. Why didn't he insist on going through the things in the attic himself? If only, but Pastor remembered what his mother used to say to him and his brother when they were growing up, 'Don't talk about what you should have done or could have done. Once something has happened, so be it, make the best of it because crying over spilled milk is senseless.'

"Detria, what I wanted your husband to understand is that I really wanted to believe that the child Audrey was carrying was mine. I wanted both of us to cling to that, to have faith even though something so terrible had happened. Plus, I didn't want her to abort an innocent child regardless of the circumstances of that child's conception."

Detria toyed with her hair nervously. "Pastor, I hear what you're saying, and part of me understands your reasoning. But Audrey was raped, Pastor. Raped," she repeated. "That's something every woman fears in her life at some point in time. And it happened to her. I can't see how she was able to deal with carrying a child to term, knowing she could probably very well be carrying the seed of a monster."

Pastor shook his head. "We had no way of knowing that. Anyway, God bought her through it. Audrey was always a strong woman. After Francesca was born we had a DNA test done, and," he paused, his body slumped as he lowered his head in obvious shame and despair. "and she wasn't my daughter, well not biologically anyway. But I loved her just like she was mine. And I thought Audrey would be able to do the same."

"And she couldn't?" questioned Detria.

"She tried. She tried real hard, but she just couldn't seem to ever really bond with Francesca. Poor Audrey. She loved me so much that she was willing to go to the ends of the earth for me. And she practically did." Pastor looked up and over toward Detria. "And I know she loved Francesca. I just know she did. I don't care what Stiles or Francesca say, I know Audrey loved her."

"Well, getting Stiles to understand that is going to be tough, not to mention when he tells Francesca about everything that happened."

"I wish you would talk to him, Detria."

"Me?" she pointed at herself "What do you want me to talk to him about? He hardly ever listens to anything I have to say, especially lately."

"What are you talking about?" Pastor asked. "What's going on with you two?"

"Pastor, I wish I knew." Detria covered her face with trembling hands. "I don't know what's happening between us." Holding her head back up she continued to talk to Pastor, telling him how Stiles had been behaving toward her lately. She conveniently left out the reasons Stiles was so upset with her.

"All he seems concerned about is Baby Audrey. I mean, since I gave birth to her, it's like I don't exist, that I'm not important. Pastor, I'm his wife," Detria seethed and gave Pastor a haunting glare. "I know I probably shouldn't be telling you this, but what do I have to lose?"

"What is it? You know you can tell me."

"He, he doesn't touch me anymore, Pastor. He acts like he's revolted by me or something. I've been doing everything I can to show him my support. Working at Holy Rock almost every day, practically all day, trying to support his vision for that church. And what do I get? Nothing. Not even one kind word."

"I don't know what to say other than I'll pray for you. I would tell you that I'd talk to Stiles, but I don't think he wants anything to do with me, at least for now he doesn't. And I can't say I blame him. But none of us are perfect, Detria. Not me, not Stiles, not you. No one. But you know what?"

"No, what?" asked Detria.

"As for my son, I've walked in his shoes. It's not an easy job, not by a long shot, being pastor, and always expected to serve others. Always being scrutinized and expected to be available twenty four seven to the needs and wants of your congregation. It's a tough assignment, real tough."

"So that gives him an excuse to be like he is toward me? Gosh, I'm his wife. Don't I deserve some of that time and attention, some of his love and affection?"

"Child, all I'm saying is we all mess up and make decisions that may not be the best for us or our loved ones at the time. But that's part of being human. Only God is perfect, but you know that already. Maybe I *am* the blame for what Audrey went through, but I wanted her to know that no one or nothing could ever make me stop loving her."

Detria stirred uneasily on the sofa. "I know you loved her. That was easy to see. And she loved you. Stiles and Francesca are just going to have to accept that what's done is done. Francesca should be grateful that she's here on this earth. Maybe her life hasn't been peaches and cream, but there are millions of people in this world walking around every day dealing with things far worse than what she's had to deal with. And Stiles, well, he should understand that Audrey Graham was a full grown woman who was capable of making decisions for herself. And her decision back then was to keep her baby, and she did."

Pastor nodded. “I’m glad you’re not jumping all over me. Thank you,” he said.

“I’m the last one to place judgment on anybody, Pastor. Look at what I did to you? But you forgave me and you treat me just like a daughter. The thought that I could abuse you the way that I did, is well, it’s unthinkable. I never thought I was capable of such a heinous act. So I don’t see how Stiles and anyone else for that matter can come off trying to judge you.”

Pastor stammered as he pushed the words from his mouth. “That’s over and done with. You were under tremendous stress back when that happened. And I, well I was conveniently in place for you to do what you did. But it’s done and over with now. I forgave you and I don’t want you bringing that up again. You hear me?” he asked.

“Yes, I hear you, Pastor. Thank you.” Detria stood up and walked over and stood next to Pastor. She looked at him, and extended her hand toward his. He accepted it, got up and stood next to her. “I better go,” she said and started walking toward the door. Pastor followed in silence.

Detria turned and faced him after she opened his front door to leave. “Pastor, get some rest. Try not to worry too much about all of this. Like the Bible says, ‘this too shall pass.’”

Pastor leaned in and kissed Detria on her left cheek. “You do the same, sweetheart. I want you to be careful going home, all right?”

“Yes, I’ll be careful.” She took a step outside and on to the porch before she stopped. “You’re going to be at church tomorrow aren’t you?”

“Yes, I’m going to church with my companion, Josie.”

"Oh, I see. Why aren't you coming to Holy Rock? I can't believe you're going to let this rift between you and Stiles keep you from coming to your own church."

"I think your husband will feel better if I'm not sitting up in the pulpit. Holy Rock will always be my home church, but right now, I think I'll visit with Josie at least for the next few Sundays. You know, wait until things quiet down a little."

"I see. Well, you know what's best. Anyway, I better get going. It's already pretty late. Goodnight, Pastor."

"Goodnight, Detria."

Detria walked away while Pastor remained standing in the doorway until she got inside her car and drove off.

◊

"Hey, I'm leaving my father-in-law's house."

"That's straight. I'm at home, so why don't you swing through here. Let me look at that pretty face of yours," Skip flirted.

Detria smiled into the phone. "I'm on my way. Bye."

"Bye."

Detria had been talking to Skip for three months. She couldn't remember how their affair started, but one thing she did know was that she was developing strong feelings for Skip more and more. He gave her the attention she craved to get from Stiles. But Stiles was in his own space, his own world and it didn't seem to include her. Detria believed he still wanted his ex and she was nothing like Rena. She smiled wickedly when she thought about the package of condoms she'd sent her. "Wonder how you liked that wedding gift Miss Rena? I can't believe you haven't called whining to my husband about it. Or who knows, you probably did, but let's see if he's going to confront me about it," she kept talking to herself.

She drove down Holmes Road until she arrived in the county. She made a left on Ross and traveled through the neighborhood until she reached her destination. She was glad Skip lived quite a distance from the church. It was less of a chance that she would be seen by those nosey Holy Rock church folk. She called Skip when she turned on to his street so he would have the garage up and she could drive right up in there undetected.

Skip closed the garage door and scooped Detria in his arms as soon as it closed completely. His lips pressed against hers with unbridled passion as his tongue explored the recesses of her mouth.

"Skip," she struggled to say but his mouth covered hers hungrily as he held on to her waist and walking backward guided her into his house.

With ease, she gently tried to push him away. "Hey, don't you want to know what happened at Pastor's?" she asked, twisting in his arms and arching her body to move from his grasp.

"Not really. All I want to know right now is do you want me as much as I want you?" He gathered her into his arms and swiftly carried her to his bedroom and undressed her while Detria buried her face in his hairy chest, totally aroused by his touch.

Skip couldn't contain himself. His desire for Detria had overcome all reason. Stiles and him may have gone back a long way, but Detria was a woman that he couldn't deny. When she first openly flirted with him at church, he tried to brush her off. But she was a woman who went after what she wanted, and when he discovered it was him, he gave into her like Samson to Delilah.

His hands moved gently and expertly up and down the length of her back. Detria welcomed him by curling into the curve of his body. Her defenses against his lovemaking weakened as she rose to meet him, without thoughts of Stiles or Baby Audrey ever entering her mind.

After their lovemaking, they lay spent in each other's arms.

"I can't lay here all night," she finally said in a faint whisper. "It's getting late."

Skip responded by kissing her again.

"Come on, Skip," she said and eased away from him. "As much as I want to stay, you know I can't. We both have to be at church early in the morning too."

Skip reluctantly released her. "Yeah, I know but we don't get to do this often, so when I do see you, I don't want it to be a pit stop. You know what I mean?"

"I know what you mean. And believe me, I don't want to leave you. But we've got to be careful. At least I have to be careful. You're a single man with nothing to worry about. Me, on the other hand, I'm the First Lady and a mother too. I can't afford to have Stiles trying to drag my name through the mud or take my daughter away from me if he finds out about us. I have a lot to lose."

"At least take a shower with me before you go."

"You drive a hard bargain, Skip Madison. How can a girl say no?"

"Come on, let me make you presentable for your husband," he said and led her into the bathroom.

"You are such a naughty boy."

"And you love it," he said and closed the door behind them.

16

"The face is the mirror of the mind, and eyes without speaking confess the secrets of the heart." Saint Jerome

Detria tip-toed up the steps. As she approached their bedroom, she saw the door was closed. She slowly turned the knob and peeped inside. The bed was empty. Leaving the door open, Detria turned and walked up the hallway toward the guest room. That door was also closed. She repeated her previous actions, only this time when she opened the door, she saw Stiles in the bed.

Turning to walk away, she halted when she heard his voice.

"Where have you been?"

Before she turned around to face him she sucked in her breath and then slowly released it. "I went to see Pastor. After all of that yelling you did over the phone, and refusing to let me in on what was going on, I went and found out for myself. And honestly, Stiles, I have to admit that I understand why you were so upset." She purposely changed her tone to sound sympathetic toward him.

Stiles sat upright in the bed and swung his legs to the side. "Is that right?"

"Of course. What could Pastor have been thinking? Why did he insist on your mother carrying the seed of another man?"

"Didn't he tell you why?" asked Stiles.

"He tried and I guess he thought he was doing what was best for him and Audrey at the time. He said when she first found out she was pregnant, they weren't sure if the baby was his or not. And you know him, he doesn't believe in abortion under any circumstance."

"I can't believe that this is the same man. The man who I've respected and loved all of these years as my father. And he turns out to be some, some kind of dictator who was remiss about what he put my mother through."

Detria walked all the way inside the guest room. "Stiles, you have to let it go. It's over and done with. And as far as telling Francesca about this, I hope you don't."

Stiles stared at his wife. "You think I'm going to keep something like this from my sister? Everything she went through growing up, she never knew the reason why. Neither did I. But now it all makes sense. I'm not saying that my mother was right to treat Francesca the way that she did, but at least I can say she had a reason. Francesca has to know so she can maybe finally close the chapter on her past. Keeping this whole thing a secret is what caused all this mess in our family in the first place."

Detria pouted her lips and released a heavy sigh. “That’s on you then. Do what you feel is best. I’m just saying that sometimes it’s best to leave the past in the past. That’s all.”

“It’s not that simple, but then you wouldn’t know anything about that, would you?” Stiles asked with bite in his voice.

“What is that supposed to mean?”

“Never mind, Detria. I don’t want to argue with you anymore. But I’m going to tell you this, don’t ever think that you’re going to get away with the little games you call yourself playing, and don’t you ever, and I mean ever leave my daughter with anybody until you talk it over with me.”

“Whatever, Stiles. I’m going to bed.” Detria abruptly swished around and walked toward the bedroom door. “Oh, and don’t you worry,” she said, “You’ll see your precious little Audrey tomorrow morning. I’ll tell Mother Brown to bring her to your office before church starts. Maybe that’ll make you feel better.”

“Me, feel better? You daggone right it’ll make me feel better. And I can’t believe you’re not concerned about how she’s doing over there tonight. She’s not in her own bed, or in familiar surroundings.”

“Well, if you were so terribly disturbed about her being with Mother Brown, like I said, you should have gone over there and picked her up. You didn’t, so it doesn’t seem like you’re too bothered. Anyway, I’m going to take advantage of her not being here and I’m going to go to bed and have an uninterrupted sleep. Goodnight.”

Detria left, went to their bedroom, undressed and climbed in the bed. *Lord, forgive me. But you know my marriage is in shambles and Skip, well, Skip treats me like a woman, like he really cares about me. And Father, you already know before I even pray to you, that my husband has turned out not to be the man of my dreams. I promise I won't sleep with Skip again. Forgive me.*

◊

Stiles settled back in the bed, his frustration mounting. He casually picked up his cell phone and noticed that he had seven voicemail messages. His first thought was to let them wait until after Sunday services tomorrow, but his second thought was what persuaded him to push the '1' button on the phone and listen to his messages.

The first three voicemail messages were from Brother Jones. "Pastor, just checking to see if you have any special instructions concerning tomorrow's services," Brother Jones basically said on all three messages.

"Not sure how I missed his calls. I must have dozed off earlier or something, or maybe I was in a yelling match with my wife," he mumbled.

The next message made Stiles fall back and take a seat on the side of the bed. It was Rena's voice on the other end. There was something about her voice that aroused him every time he heard it. His complexion turned a shade darker when he heard her going off on him about a box of condoms he'd sent her as a wedding gift.

Stiles had no idea what she was talking about. The more he listened to her practically cussing him out on the phone, the more he thought that Francesca had been up to her old scheming, conniving tricks again.

"Dang, why can't you just leave the woman alone, Francesca?" he looked at the time on his cell phone. "Eleven o'clock," he said. He pecked the area code and then stopped and ended the call. *Are you crazy? The woman is getting married or just got married, whatever, man. You can't just up and call her,* he told himself.

Rena, Rena, Rena, if only I could turn back the hands of time, then you'd still be mine. He tossed and turned as he tried to relax in the bed, but it was of no use. He reminisced about the good times he'd shared with Rena during their courtship. He thought about her smile, her sense of naïveté, and her devotion toward him. But his thoughts also turned toward how she had deceived him. But if he could forgive Detria, why had it been impossible for him to forgive Rena? If he had, maybe his mind wouldn't keep yo-yoing back and forth.

If he could let go of what he once had with Rena, and concentrate on making his marriage work with Detria then things would be better for him, Detria and the child they had together.

Stiles got back out of the bed and dropped to his knees. There, kneeling by the side of the bed, he began to pray. "Father, God, I need your help. I'm in trouble, and I don't know where to run. I'm confused, Lord, but I know confusion is not from you. Help me to find common ground with my wife. Help me to do what I tell others to do over and over again, to let go of the past. I need to be a good husband and father, Lord. I can't effectively lead your people if I can't manage my own household."

He got up off his knees and got back in the bed. He didn't stay there long before he decided to get up and go to his own bedroom and sleep next to his wife. If there was going to be any hope of making this marriage work, it had to begin with him, he reasoned. He was the man, the head of his household, and it was time for him to get things back on track.

Stiles eased in the bed and scooted up next to Detria.

“Oh, so you decided to come in here and keep me up all night? I told you, Stiles, I don’t want to argue. I’ll get the baby in the morning. Now , please, I’m tired. I want to get some sleep,” Detria said without turning over to face him.

“Detria, look at me,” Stiles said and gently pulled her by her shoulder and turned her toward him.

Detria stared in silence.

“I know things between us have been, well jacked up to say the least. And I want to be the first to say that I’m sorry. I’m sorry for making you afraid of me. I’m sorry for my short temper and for not realizing that you have a lot on you. It’s not easy taking care of a baby. I know that. And if you’ve found someone who’ll love and take care of our daughter when you’re tired and just need some ‘me’ time then who am I to get all bent out of shape. I mean, I know that Mother Brown is a good, Christian woman. She nor Brother Brown would ever do anything to hurt our child. So, I’m sorry. I’m sorry for everything. Tell me that you forgive me,” Stiles said.

Detria shifted her weight so she was resting on her elbows. “Stiles, look, you have to trust me. I love our daughter just as much as you do. And you know I would never leave her in the hands of strangers. I could have taken her over to my parents’ house but you and I both know that they’re not in the best of health. And my sister, well she loves it when I take Audrey to see them. But the reason I took her over to Mother Brown’s was because I knew she would bring her to church tomorrow morning. You know we can never be sure if momma and daddy will be there or not, and Brooke would have taken her to her church. I know you wouldn't like that, so I asked Mother Brown to keep her. And then this sudden jealous streak you have, well it's frightening, Stiles. I have to tell you; I've never seen you behave like you have these past weeks. I've never known you to be violent. It's like you don't trust me."

"I do trust you, Detria. I really do."

"I'm not Rena, Stiles. And I'm tired of living in her shadow. I hear what you're saying but your actions say otherwise. Sometimes I feel like you're still in love with her. And if you are, then I can't compete with that. I won't compete with that, I should say."

"Baby, please. Let's start over. Let's start over right now," Stiles said. He leaned in, placed his arm underneath Detria's back and pulled her almost naked body close to his. His lips brushed the side of her cheeks before he slowly trailed kisses along the nape of her neck, down to her shoulders to her perfectly formed mounds.

Detria flinched. *I can't let him do this. Not after being with Skip*. But Detria didn't try to stop him. Instead she allowed herself to relax in his arms. She wrapped both of her arms around his neck and kissed him fully on his thick, soft lips.

Stiles' body responded completely. As he explored his wife's almost perfectly shaped body, he dismissed thoughts of Rena that tried to invade his mind. Hearing Detria's soft, sexy love cries, and caressing her soft, warm skin took him to the place he needed to be and wanted to be for some time: in the arms of his wife. His manhood connected with her body until all he could feel was his desire being fully met. This was how it was supposed to be. With each kiss, each touch, each stroke Stiles forgot the problems between him and Detria.

"You're so sweet," he whispered. "So, so sweet. And I'm sorry, baby. I'm sorry," he kept saying as he made love to his wife.

"It's going to be all right. Everything is going to be all right," she said between moans and barely above a faint whisper. "Yes, everything is going to be good." *Skip, Stiles. God. Lord, I didn't want this to happen. I shouldn't have let this happen. God, why did I let this happen?* Detria thought as cries of pleasure escaped from her lips.

17

"Woman was taken out of man; not out of his head to top him, nor out of his feet to be trampled underfoot; but out of his side to be equal to him, under his arm to be protected, and near his heart to be loved." Unknown

"Babe, why don't you and the baby ride with me to Jackson? We can stop somewhere and have a nice lunch on our way back home. You know, make it like a mini road trip," Stiles suggested over a breakfast of eggs, grits, bacon, toast and a cold, tall glass of freshly squeezed orange juice.

Detria sat in the chair across from him and Baby Audrey was in her highchair stuffing grits inside her mouth with her chubby caramel colored fingers. "Do you think Francesca is even going to want to see Audrey, or me, once she hears what you have to tell her?"

"Sure she will. Think about it. The last time she saw li'l Audrey she was just a couple of months old. Well, she's seen her through picture mail, but that's not the same as holding daddy's sweetpea in person," he replied and looked over at Baby Audrey.

"I don't know, Stiles. I don't want to go up there with you and then find myself in the middle of a big fight between you two. I mean, telling her that she was conceived during a rape, and that Pastor is not her father that's going to be tough. Real tough. Lord knows, I wouldn't want to be in your shoes, and I sure wouldn't want to be in hers."

Stiles crumbled his crispy bacon into his buttered grits and then mixed in his scrambled eggs. "To be honest, I could use the company. I don't like being the bearer of bad news myself, but I feel like it's only right that I tell her. I promise we won't stay long. And Francesca already told me that she and Tim have plans later this afternoon. But I think seeing Baby Audrey and you will help cushion the blow."

"Ummm, I don't know, Stiles," Detria responded. "But then again I guess it won't hurt. It sure can't make matters any worse if me and the baby go. And maybe you are right. Francesca probably will enjoy seeing her niece. Let's hope so anyway."

Stiles eased his body half way off the dining room chair and leaned in to kiss Detria on her lips. "Thanks, babe."

Detria got up from the table.

"Aren't you going to finish that bowl of fruit?" Stiles asked.

"Not right now. If we're going to go, I need to get dressed, get the baby ready and then get her bag packed."

"Okay. But soon as I finish eating, I'll get the baby ready. You just concentrate on you."

"Ohhh, well, that definitely sounds like a plan." Detria smiled. "It won't take me long," she said.

The house phone started ringing. "I'll get it," Stiles yelled so Detria could hear him. "Hello," he said when he picked up the phone. He already read the caller ID; it was Pastor on the other end.

"Good morning, son," Pastor said, his voice full of caution.

"Good morning," Stiles answered, not adding anything else.

"Is that my baby I hear trying to talk?" Pastor asked.

"Yes, she's calling her dada," Stiles answered with obvious pride. "What can I do for you this morning?" His voice returning to a serious tone.

"Son, I hope you've had some time to calm down and think rationally about everything that happened last week. I know it's hard for you to deal with, but you're a grown man now. And there are some things you as a man, especially a man of God that you should understand."

Stiles acted like he didn't hear Pastor. Instead he answered, "I don't have time to talk about this this morning. We're getting ready to go to Jackson.

"So, I guess you're going through with ruining the rest of your sister's life. Don't you think she's been through enough?" Pastor asked, sounding quite irritated with Stiles.

"Yes, she's been through enough, and I wonder why? It wouldn't be because you had a huge hand in making her life as miserable as it was," he bit back.

"Look, I'm not about to go there with you this morning. It's far too early and I'm not going to let the devil steal my joy."

"Oh, so now you want to bring God into this."

"God is always in the forefront of my thoughts and my actions. It's because of God's lead that I thought it was best that your mother did what she did. And I don't regret it. Not one bit."

"I'm going to let you go. I can't listen to any more of your self-righteous banter, Pastor"

"You know the Word, son. And you also know two wrongs don't make a right. If your mother had aborted your sister, we wouldn't be having this conversation. And I know you aren't on the phone telling me that you'd rather she had. If you are saying that, then maybe it's time you reevaluate your walk with the Lord."

Stiles was heated now. He couldn't believe Pastor would question his relationship with God. He was raised up in the church, a preacher's kid and all of the gut and glory that went along with it. He learned about God for himself after being spiritually steered and fed the gospel. He didn't regret it either. He was glad that he'd been raised by a godly mother like Audrey was to him and a stepfather like Pastor who truly was an anointed man of God. Until now. Now Stiles felt like he had been deceived, betrayed all of these years. His family was based on a lie. And yes, he was glad he had his sister. He didn't want anyone to ever think otherwise, but it was still the principle of the thing. Pastor, in his eyes was a hypocrite. He didn't care how much Bible he quoted or memorized, he let his wife down, his family down and in Stiles's eyes he had let God down.

"You go on up there and see where it gets you. All you're going to do is cause more dissension in this family. Francesca is finally healing not only physically but mentally. She's been given a second chance at life, a chance to make things better than they have been. And now because you're upset with me, and a decision I made that had nothing to do with you, you want to run up there and cause misery all over again in her life. Seems to me like you're the one who needs to have a little talk with Jesus," Pastor scoffed.

The doorbell rang, much to Pastor's relief. "Son, do what you feel you have to do. I've got to go." He hung up the phone.

Stiles bit his bottom lip. He went into the family room. Detria was watching the morning news while Baby Audrey was strapped in her car seat that was seated on the floor a few feet away from her.

She squirmed like she was trying desperately to break loose from the straps that held her in place.

Stiles became even more furious as he watched Detria ignore their daughter. It looked like they were ready, but Detria still acted like the baby wasn't even in the room. He walked over to Baby Audrey, and scooped up the car seat.

"It's going to be fine, sweetpea. I know you don't want to be in this ole' thing, but daddy's about to take you on a road trip. We're going to have fun," he said to his little girl.

Audrey reached for Stiles, still struggling to get out. Stiles sat the seat on the end of the sofa and balanced it there with his knee while he used his hands to release his daughter.

Detria finally looked at the two of them, but Stiles noticed a commercial had come on.

"Why are you taking her out of her car seat? Aren't you ready to go? You said we had to be up there before noon. It's," she looked at her phone, "seven fifteen."

"I guess you didn't notice that she wanted out of this thing," he answered.

"She's a child, Stiles. She can't have everything she wants, and anyway, she was just fine. It's not like sitting in a car seat was killing her. Jeez, you can be so over the top sometimes," Detria remarked.

"Just take her car seat and diaper bag while I carry her to the car." He tried to remain calm, hold back his anger. He didn't want the day to start out worse than it already had. His words with Pastor were enough, and now Detria was about to make him shoot off. But if he was going to make an effort to make things better in his marriage he was going to have to bite his tongue about a lot of things.

Detria seemed to have a way of pushing his buttons, the wrong buttons for that matter, but today he opted for a simpler solution rather than going off on her. That was to do just what he'd done – carry his daughter in his arms without making a huge fuss about his wife's lack of motherly affection toward their child.

Detria used the remote to power down the flat screen before she retrieved the diaper bag parked next to her on the sofa. She stood and then walked over and grabbed hold of the car seat.

"Let's go," she ordered.

◊

"Good morning, early bird," Pastor said as he opened the door for Josie, his neighbor and companion. The couple officially became an item shortly after

Francesca and Tim's wedding. Pastor enjoyed Josie's company. She was spry, energetic, loved the Lord and her church, loved her family and she reminded him of Audrey in many ways. Like Audrey, she catered to his every need. She came this morning baring two containers filled with food. Pastor already knew whatever was inside was delicious. He hated to admit it, but Josie was probably a better cook than his Audrey had been.

"Step aside and let me in," she said. "It's already getting hot out there." She walked into the apartment like she was at home, and headed toward his kitchen.

"What you got there?" he asked, a smile formed on his face. He was glad Josie had arrived when she did. He had grown weary of Stiles' attacks and if he had remained on the phone a little longer, he may have said some things that he might regret later.

"I made some rice, sausage and biscuit this morning. You haven't eaten yet, have you?" She stated more than questioned.

"No, I haven't. And you know me too well, Josie," Pastor said in a flirtatious tone. "I was about to fix me a bowl of instant oatmeal."

"Well, now you don't have to. I'll put it on a plate for you. Everything's still good and hot so you don't have to put it in the microwave."

She opened the dishwasher and removed a plate, fork and a large spoon. "Do you want me to scramble you a couple of eggs right quick?" she asked.

"Umm, you don't have to. Rice and sausage is enough."

"That means yes," she replied. "It won't take me but a minute. You can go on and do what you were doing. Put your clothes on or something. I thought you would be out of your pajamas by now. You usually are this time of morning," she told him.

"Yeah, I know, but my son called and that threw off my routine a little. "

"Oh, is everything all right with Stiles and his family?"

"Yes, everything's fine," he said. He cared deeply about Josie. Trusted her too, but he was not about to share his family secrets with her. "He was just telling me that the three of them are going to go see Francesca this morning."

"Oh, that's nice." Josie opened the refrigerator, removed two eggs, a stick of butter, and the pint sized container of skimmed milk, a tomato and some sharp cheddar. Next, she looked in the cabinet over the sink and removed a small glass bowl. She cracked the two eggs, then added measured portions of milk, salt and pepper, diced up part of the tomato, sliced some of the cheese and scrambled it all together in the bowl. "I love it when couples spend quality time together. It's good for a marriage. Any relationship really," she said while she prepared the food.

"Um hum. I'll be right back. While you're doing that, I'm going back here and put on my clothes. They're already lying out on my bed, so it won't take me but a minute."

"That's fine. Everything will be ready when you get back." Josie proceeded to sing while she turned on the stove, put the skillet on top of the burner and waited on it to heat up before adding the scrambled mixture.

"I sing because I'm happy. I sing because I'm freeee," she sang in perfect pitch. Josie loved to sing. She was one of the lead singers in her church choir.

Pastor had invited her to perform a solo at Holy Rock several months ago during women's month. It was another one of the things that endeared him to Josie. When she sang, as she often did when she was around him, it had a way of soothing his spirit. Somehow it made him forget about the troubles and worries of the day.

He returned to the kitchen a few minutes later fully dressed and patting his flat belly. "Where's my food, woman?" he said jokingly.

"Man, don't you start me up this morning," she said placing both hands on her thick hips. "You won't get not one bit of this food if you mess with me."

He walked up to her, his gait still uneven, residual and lasting effects of his last stroke. His arms wrapped around her waist then moved around her back side. His lips met hers and without pause, he kissed her.

Josie reciprocated. Both arms held on to him as she reached up and encircled his neck. He stood several inches taller than her, yet he would be described as vertically challenged by most people. But petite Josie considered him tall in her book. Her late husband, who died a year before Audrey, had been a big and tall man. He would have towered at least a foot over Pastor.

"I love to hear you sing," he told her when he pulled away. "Your voice is like an angel singing from heaven."

Josie blushed. "Thank you, Pastor. It's just a gift the good Lord gave me, and I intend to use it until He calls me home."

Pastor pulled out a chair and sat down at the breakfast table. "Are you going to join me?" he asked.

Josie plated the food and sat it on the table in front of Pastor. "I already ate, but I am going to have a cup of orange juice." She returned to the refrigerator and pulled the carton of orange juice out of the fridge and poured her and Pastor a glass before she sat down across from him.

"Do you have anything special planned for today?"

"I'm going to sort through those boxes Stiles bought over here the other day. And later on, I said I might drive up to the Dollar General. I need to get a few items for around the house. Would you care to join me?"

"I don't know. What time are you going?"

"You know it won't be until after Judge Mathis goes off. So, I'll say about noon. What, you have something planned?"

"Nothing other than watching Judge Mathis with you, and when I leave here this morning I'm going to go home and put a load of clothes in the washer. That's all. So I'll go with you."

Pastor ate his food. "This is delicious," he complimented. "These eggs are the best." He reached across the table and patted her hand.

"Thank you." Josie took a swallow of her juice while she watched him eat.

Their relationship was a good one. Both of them had survived the death of their spouses, both of them had battled with illnesses. Pastor and his strokes. Josie and her rheumatoid arthritis. But together they strengthened each other in more ways than from a physical aspect.

Pastor was a good listener. Josie surmised it was because of his profession. As a Pastor over the years he'd had to listen to an endless list of people who sought his counsel and prayers. She was impressed with his patience and understanding. He wasn't judgmental at all. She could honestly say, if she had to, that she'd grown to love Pastor, and she believed he loved her as well. She was grateful to God for blessing her with a companion in her golden years as was Pastor.

Pastor finished eating his breakfast, leaned back in the chair and took the final swallow of juice. “Ahhh, I’m stuffed,” he said.

“Good.” She got up from the table. “I’m going to leave you for a while. I’ll be back by eleven. Do you want me to bring you anything back when I come?” she asked.

“No, just you. That’s all I need.”

“Pastor, stop it. You’re being mighty fresh this morning,” she said.

“Just telling you what God loves, the truth.” He stood up too and as he did, he reached out and took hold of her hand, bought it up to his lips and planted tiny feather like kisses on her hand and wrist. “You want to hang around until Judge Mathis comes on? You can put clothes in the washer anytime,” he said.

“And you can go through boxes anytime,” she replied.

“Say no more then.” He stretched out his arm, and Josie smiled, as she walked toward the bedroom door instead of the front door.

Pastor stood back. Silence filled the room as he watched her hips sway like palm trees. He smiled with satisfaction.

18

"What is a cynic? A man who knows the price of everything and the value of nothing." Oscar Wilde

"Good morning, Tim," Stiles said and walked inside Tim and Francesca's house with a fussing Baby Audrey in his arms and a quiet, tight-lipped wife next to him. "How's it going, my man? It's been a while since I last saw you."

"Yeah, it has. But everything's good. Me and Francesca are fine, aren't we baby?" Tim said and turned to Francesca who stood next to him, looking as sullen as Detria.

"Uh huh," she replied as she shifted her eyes toward Detria. "Hi, Detria."

"Hello, Francesca. You're looking well," Detria remarked.

"Thanks," she said and then focused her attention on Baby Audrey. "Look at you, little woman. You are growing so fast," she said and lightly pinched the bouncing baby's fat cheeks. "She is cute as a button."

"Thanks, sis. I think she has your big brown eyes. What do you think?" he asked proudly.

"I think you're talking out the side of your neck," Francesca answered.

"Talking out the side of your neck?" Detria scowled. "What does that mean?"

Francesca threw up her hands, giving Detria a questioning look. "Nothing. It means nothing. Just a little slang. Y'all come on in," she offered.

"Yeah, come inside," Tim added. "Go on back in the family room. That's where we usually hang out."

"This place is nice," complimented Stiles as his eyes surveyed the well decorated space. He gave the credit to Francesca. She had always been a neat freak and good at making anything look good.

"Yeah, it sure is nice," Detria added as they both looked around while being escorted through the 2300 hundred square foot home.

Tim and Francesca had their dream home built from the ground up. They'd been in the house over six months, but this was the first time Stiles had seen it. Francesca never invited him or Pastor to come up and Stiles had learned that if he wasn't invited, then there was no need to invite himself because Francesca would find some excuse to brush him off. This time was different because Stiles was determined to not only tell her about Pastor and Audrey, but he wanted to see if he could somehow find some private time to ask her why she sent those box of condoms to Rena and then pretended like he had sent them. On the one hand he hated the way Audrey had treated his sister, but then on the other hand he was sick of Francesca's vindictive, revenge seeking ways.

"Would you like something to eat? Drink?" Tim asked the couple.

"Not me," Stiles answered then looked over at his wife.

"Yes, water please."

"Anything for the little princess?" Tim looked at Baby Audrey and chuckled as she planted slobbery kisses on her daddy's face.

"No, I have her juice cup and food in the bag. I'll give her that after her daddy changes her pamper."

Detria sat down on one end of the red sectional that was positioned to face a big window and two small windows, and opened the diaper bag. She took a pamper out the bag and passed it to Stiles without so much as blinking an eye. "Here."

Stiles looked at her, accepted the pamper and then turned to Francesca who's eyes were glued on the two of them. "Where can I change her?" he asked.

Francesca pointed behind her. "Go up that hall and take a right. Second door on the left is the bathroom. "

"Thanks, sis," he said and disappeared with Baby Audrey still bouncing and chattering in his arms.

Detria seemed to be growing more and more detached from Baby Audrey, but Stiles tried to ignore his mounting concern. Some women were more career oriented than others. Maybe Detria fell into that category. He wanted to blame it on anything other than her being a bad mother. That was something he couldn't fathom.

Sties walked back into the family room with Baby Audrey holding on to his shirt, and looking like she was in seventh heaven. She was just nine months old but she already displayed signs of being a 'daddy's girl' and Stiles ate it up. He adored his daughter and his dreams were to have more children with Detria, but with each day that passed, and the mounting tension growing in their marriage, Stiles was becoming more uncertain about that possibility.

"Okay, Stiles what is it that was so important that you had to drive up here to tell me?" Francesca asked, cutting through any chance of making small talk with him. She was glad to see her little niece, but Francesca didn't want to prolong their visit. She welcomed her privacy and her new life with Tim and his family. Stiles and Pastor would only bring confusion and turmoil in her life, and she didn't want or need that. Prime example, he practically insisted on coming to their new home in Jackson, Tennessee to upset her. Francesca knew that would be the case because if it was anything good or positive that he had to say, her brother would have told her over the phone, or not at all. Seemed like her family was only good for making her life miserable and she was sick and tired of it. She'd already told Tim when they first got up that morning, that she was done dealing with Stiles and Pastor unless it was a real family crisis.

Pastor may have been her father, and she loved him dearly, but she had made up in her mind to love him from afar. As for Stiles, of course she loved him. He was her blood, her brother. But some of his ways reminded her of Audrey. He could be self-seeking and at times he blamed her for the problems she'd encountered in her life. It was like he was the perfect one, always had been in the eyes of Audrey, but Francesca knew that Stiles had a violent streak that hardly anyone knew about. But she did. She'd been the recipient of his back slaps, trip ups, and nasty verbal assaults when they were growing up. But like always, Audrey never stood up for her. She always took Stiles' side no matter what. She could be bleeding from a hit or fall that was caused by her brother, but Audrey somehow managed to turn it around and blame her for it.

With Audrey being dead, Francesca felt like she could finally breathe; finally live a rather normal life even though she had been diagnosed with AIDS. But even her AIDS diagnosis wasn't scary to Francesca anymore. She'd been following the advice of the village doctor.

Overall, she had started feeling better. She had learned so much from their trip to Honduras. For a long time she didn't quite grasp the difference in being HIV positive and having AIDS. Now she understood that HIV meant she had the virus and could pass it on to others like her darling husband, Tim. But the two of them practiced safe sex and believed in the power of God to protect Tim. As for being diagnosed with AIDS, Francesca also learned AIDS was not a single disease, but it was comprised of a variety of diseases that was caused by reduced immunity. In simpler terms, she was more likely to develop opportunistic infections. But she was a fighter, and was determined not to give up on her battle against the virus. She was following the program suggested to her by the self-proclaimed doctor and was determined to follow whatever regimen possible in order to strengthen her ability to fight off infection and restore her immune function.

She had come to the realization since meeting Tim that she really wanted to live. Her faith in God had increased a hundred fold. Every day she quoted Psalm one eighteen verse seventeen that she kept pinned on her master bathroom mirror: "I will not die but live, and will proclaim what the LORD has done.' She was more in tune with her body and making herself whole again. She wanted to prepare herself to have a family.

Tim and Francesca had approached the subject of having children. It was one of the main reasons for Tim's decision to move out of Newbern and settle in Jackson which was closer to family and friends. Plus, their church was in Jackson too.

Everything was falling into place for Francesca and Tim. Life couldn't be better – until Stiles told Francesca about Audrey and Pastor.

Francesca listened to Stiles as he sat on the sofa holding a now sleeping Baby Audrey. He slowly and deliberately gave her the details of his findings and shared Pastor's reaction about the whole situation. Francesca felt like she'd been punched dead square in the gut after listening to Stiles.

"I don't want to hear anymore," she suddenly screamed, waking up Baby Audrey who started screaming too. Francesca covered both ears, stood up and limped as fast as she could out of the room.

Detria's mouth flung open and Stiles looked stunned as he passed the crying baby to Detria and stood up like he was going to go after Francesca.

Tim stopped him by jumping up and positioning himself in front of Stiles. Tim, though inches shorter than Stiles, appeared larger than life. His anger was obvious. "So this is what you came up here to do. You just had to come up here and upset my wife, didn't you, Stiles?" Tim shouted as he stood toe to toe with Stiles. He had listened with trepidation to Stiles as he told Francesca about Pastor and Audrey, the rape, and the way she was conceived.

"I want you out of here," Tim ordered pointing toward the other direction that would lead outside. "Get out of here now," he yelled above crying Audrey. Detria grabbed hold of the diaper bag and swiftly turned and walked toward the front of the house.

"Let's go," she said. "Let's go now," she said again. "You've done enough here."

Stiles looked at her like she was crazy but he followed behind her. As soon as they made it outside, Stiles felt the wind of the steel door against his back as Tim slammed it shut.

"Guess you're happy now, huh?" Detria mocked. "You've managed to totally alienate your one and only sister. I knew in my gut that this was a bad idea. I just knew it was," she repeated as she roughly strapped Baby Audrey in her car seat.

Stiles didn't say a word. His fury could be seen in the twitch of his jaw line and the deep crease in his forehead.

They got in the car. Stiles turned the ignition, put the car in reverse before turning and speeding down the secluded street lined with magnificent dogwood trees.

Neither of them said a word for at least ten minutes. Stiles drove , his jaw still flinching as he thought about how disastrous his visit had turned out. He looked at the clock on the console. "You want to stop here?" he asked as he pulled into a Chick fil-a restaurant. "You can get you a salad or fruit cup."

"Don't bother. I'm not hungry. I just want to go home. I hope you realize the damage you've done, Stiles."

"Look, don't start with me, Detria," he yelled.

"I did what I thought was best.. I knew she would be upset but I had no idea she would take it as hard as she did. You act like I wanted to see my sister hurt."

"Well?" Detria shot back.

"Well, what? You know I'm sick of you and your negativity. Where is the supportive, kind, loving woman I first met? Where is she, Detria?"

"Shuuu, I could ask you the same question. Where is the sweet, sensitive, considerate and loving man I met? I sure don't see any traces of him now."

Stiles turned the car around and headed back out into traffic and on to the interstate. He didn't stop driving until he made it back home to Memphis. So much for spending quality time with his wife and daughter.

He rubbed his head back and forth. *Lord, I need to hear from you. I need to hear a rhema word from you real bad. Real bad and real fast.*

◊

Tim tapped on the door to their bedroom before opening it and walking inside. Francesca lay quietly, curled up in a fetal position. Tim listened to her cries. He felt her pain. Walking over to the bed, he slowly sat down, planting himself behind Francesca.

With tenderness he began massaging her back in a circular motion as he leaned down and kissed the side of her face.

"Baby, I'm so sorry. If I had known he was coming up here to tell you the mess he did, you better believe he never would have stepped foot in this house. I'm so sorry, so sorry," he continued.

Francesca continued to weep, something she would never do if she was still living the life of the old Francesca. Crying to her was a sign of weakness and she wasn't weak by any means. But with Tim, she could be totally open and exposed. She turned toward him and buried her face against his thigh while he stroked her hair and wiped away her tears.

"Why? How? Tim, I'm nothing am I? Nothing," she said again.

"Don't say that, sweetheart. You know better than that. You're a beautiful woman. I love you and nothing, and I do mean nothing Stiles said, or anything Pastor did can change that. All of that stuff he came up here with is junk. It means nothing."

Francesca looked up, her eyes already swelling from crying so hard. "But it does mean something, Tim. It means a whole lot. What is it with me? Why do people seem to want to hurt me over and over again? And Audrey, why did she listen to Pastor? Why didn't she just kill me like she wanted to do in the first place? Then I wouldn't be going through all of this. I'm tired, Tim. I can't fight anymore."

Tim caressed her chin. "Yes, you can. You're a fighter and you know it. I don't know why Stiles felt he had to tell you the stuff he did. I don't know why your father imposed his opinions on Audrey. And I don't know why Audrey felt like she couldn't stand up against him. All I know is that I'm so glad she didn't abort you. I'm so glad you're here. I know you've been through a lot, Francesca, and I can't begin to tell you how sorry I am for all the pain you've endured throughout your life. But I can say that I'm so grateful I found you. So grateful we found each other." He grabbed hold of Francesca by the shoulders and gently lifted her up toward him until she was face to face with him. He kissed her first gently and then with full force. “I love you. I love you so much,” he said as he pulled away and looked into her tear filled eyes. “I promise, I‘ll never let him near you again. I’ll never let them hurt you again.”

They embraced and Francesca finally took a deep breath and then slowly, she exhaled.

“I love you, Tim.”

“I know you do. Now why don’t you lay on down. I’ll go make us some breakfast and then I’ll bring your morning meds. How about that?”

Francesca nodded.

Tim stood up and then before leaving he bent down and kissed Francesca on the top of her head. “I’ll be back.”

Francesca balled back up in a knot. As she replayed everything Stiles had told her, her hurt turned into a slow evolving ember of fire. Why her? Why did it always have to be her that people wanted to hurt?

Francesca decided that she had to talk to Pastor for herself. She had to hear his explanation. She turned over and reached for the landline. She wanted to call Pastor but she remembered she didn’t know his number. *Maybe that’s a sign that I need to see him face to face. I want to see the look on his face when he tells me what really happened.*

She got up and walked into the kitchen where Tim was making preparations to cook, something else he loved to do.

“Hey, you. I thought I told you to lie down and rest,” he said when he saw his wife enter their industrial styled kitchen.

“I want to go to Memphis, Tim.”

Tim stopped doing what he was doing and looked at his wife. “Memphis? For what?”

“I need to see Pastor,” she said before turning and walking away.

19

"*What you need to know about the past is that no matter what has happened, it has all worked together to bring you to this very moment. And this is the moment you can choose to make everything new. Right now.*" *Unknown*

Her period was late, and she felt bloated and cranky. *Could I be pregnant? What if I am? Will my baby have herpes?* She drove to the Walgreens on the corner to purchase a pregnancy test kit. *No need in getting Robert excited if it's a false alarm.*

She wanted a child with Robert so badly, and he was down with the idea of having another child too. When the test came back with a positive reading, she was both nervous and happy.

When she told Robert about the test results he was elated. He reassured her that no matter what, he would be by her side, and everything would be just fine.

"Make an appointment, and let's make sure the test you took is right. I can't believe I'm going to be a father again."

"Oh, Robert, I can't believe it. What if I really am pregnant?" she gasped with excitement fully evident in her voice.

"God knows we've been trying," Robert said and burst into laughter.

"You are so crazy," Rena remarked. "I'll call Dr. Elmore today to see when I can get in to see her."

"Good, you do that," Robert told her and pat her on the butt.

◇

"The test was definitely right," Dr. Elmore informed Rena as she sat on the exam table.

"Oh, my gosh. I'm pregnant. I'm really, really pregnant. Robert, oh, Robert." She extended her arms, and Robert stood up and walked into them.

"Yes, we are going to have ourselves a little one," he said and hugged her.

"Doctor, is my baby going to be okay? I mean you know with me..."

"With her having herpes, how can it affect our child," Robert finished.

"I don't want you to worry about that," Dr. Elmore told the couple. "I'm telling you, Mrs. Becton that your baby is likely to be absolutely fine. Since you already had herpes before you got pregnant, and you say you've had it for a few years, your body has had time to make antibodies to the virus, and that immunity is passed to the baby while he or she," she said and smiled, "is growing on the inside of you. "That's not to say that you won't incur outbreaks during your pregnancy because it's possible that you will."

Rena's smile turned into a straight face. "But I haven't had an outbreak in over a year?"

"I understand, and that's great, but I still have to inform you of the possibility. You have every reason to be ecstatic, Mrs. Becton. You can still give birth to a normal, healthy, uninfected baby, as long as certain medical precautions are taken. So, I want you to take your prenatal vitamins, and I'm also writing you a prescription for nausea too. Eat healthy and I'll see you in a month. Until then, enjoy being pregnant."

Rena and Robert left Dr. Elmore's office with huge grins on their faces.

"I can't believe it, Robert," she said with excitement resonating off each word she spoke. "We're pregnant. I'm pregnant," she said and pointed at herself before she stopped on the sidewalk and planted a whopping kiss on Robert's lips.

He in turn picked her up and twirled her around. "Didn't I tell you that everything was going to be all right?" he said when he stopped twirling her. "Wait until the kids hear about this. They're going to be happy as can be."

"Uh, I don't know. They might be jealous."

"Please, you know how much they love playing with each other, not to mention they're like the ultimate social butterflies, "he teased.

"Yes, you're right. Oh, Robert I can't wait to tell everybody. I'm so happy. God has smiled down on me, on us. And I promise you that I'm going to do everything I can to make sure we do have a happy, healthy baby. Any and everything Dr. Elmore tells me to do, I'm doing."

They got in the car and Robert, before turning the ignition switch, took hold of her hand and pressed a kiss in her palm. “You have made me the happiest man in the world once again.”

Rena eased back against the passenger window. “Uh, what do you mean by once again,” she asked him all while a smile formed on her face.

“Well, you made me happy when I first laid eyes on you. I thought you were the most beautiful woman on the face of the earth. The second time was when you agreed to marry me and now the third time is definitely the charm because you’re having my baby. Now, are you satisfied?”

“Yes. Very,” she answered as her heart swelled with joy.

◊

“You sure you want to do this?”

“Very sure. If I don’t do it now, I might not ever do it. I want to hear it for myself,” Francesca told Tim as they drove along Interstate 40 West toward Memphis.

“You know I can still turn around. I don’t want you putting yourself through unnecessary pain, Francesca. Plus, you know and I know that we have to take every precaution to keep you well. And added stress is definitely not good.”

“Will you stop it, Tim? I’m not stressing. I’m anxious, maybe, but not stressed. All I want to do is hear the truth straight from the horse’s mouth and not from Audrey’s male clone.”

“Male clone? That’s a little biting don’t you think?” Tim asked and sneaked a quick peek at his wife before returning his attention to the road.

“Nope. It’s the truth. That’s exactly what he is.”

Tim shrugged his shoulders. "Okay, whatever you say." He continued driving, taking his time to watch the other drivers who seemed to be in a hurry to get to wherever they were going.

Francesca turned up the radio when she heard her one of her all time favorite R&B songs. She loved all types of music including some rap, although contemporary gospel was her favorite. But today, she wanted to listen to something that would keep her pumped and Beyonce's Love On Top fit the bill to a tee. She started singing along and poking Tim in the side at the same time. *"Baby, it's you," she sang. "You're the one I love. You're the one..."* she sang and kept poking him.

"All right now. Sing it, girl. Sing it to daddy." Tim laughed.

"Whoa, did you just call yourself 'daddy'?" Francesca started laughing uncontrollably, leaning all against the car door.

"What's wrong with that? You don't think I fit the bill or something?"

"Boy, please."

They continued laughing and talking along the way. Tim was glad to hear his wife's laughter instead of listening to her crying over in the night like she'd been doing ever since Stiles' visit the week before. Stiles had called several times after then, but Tim refused to allow him to talk to Francesca. In Tim's eyes Stiles had done enough damage already, and he was determined not to allow Stiles or anyone else to hurt his wife again.

Tim really did not want to drive Francesca to Memphis, but she had hounded him so that he thought it was better to bring her than have her sitting around the house moping and crying. He had prayed about it and came to the conclusion that it was better if she talked to Pastor and maybe then she would find some closure. He wanted her life to be as peaceful as possible knowing that her health could take a drastic and deadly turn at any time. She was a trooper, a real trooper but Tim was realistic too. One little sneeze or a cold could turn into a death call for Francesca so he was protective over her and watched her like a hawk.

It was one of the reasons he had gone back to school shortly after they got married. He wanted to be able to provide a good life for his wife but he also wanted to have a job that would allow him to work from home most of the time. He'd achieved those things. His job as a web designer was flexible, and he enjoyed being his own boss. Like his father, he prided himself on being an entrepreneur. He had attended and finished ITT Tech and became proficient in website design, and was now making a pretty lucrative income all from the comfort of the home he shared with Francesca.

"Do you want to stop somewhere and get a bite to eat?" he asked Francesca who had stopped singing and was laid back in the slightly reclined front seat.

"I'm good. But if you want to stop somewhere, go ahead. I know you didn't eat much lunch."

"No, I'm good too. We have some granola bars in that bag on the back seat. I put one of your fruit cups in there too."

"Oh, that was nice of you. You're so good to me, Tim." She lifted her head slightly and looked over at her husband.

"You make it easy," he said and glanced quickly over at her.

"I wonder what he's going to say, Tim. I mean, do you think Pastor is going to fess up and tell me the truth? Or do you think he's going to be so shocked to see me that he's going to play the silent role?"

"Well, he's definitely going to be surprised to see you. I mean, he hasn't seen you in months and it's not like you talk to the man that much either. But that just might work in your favor."

"What do you mean?"

"He may be so shocked that he won't have time to lie. And I'm sure Stiles told him how things went down so that's even more reason for him to believe that he won't be hearing from you anytime soon."

"I just want to confront him. Get the truth straight from him. The whole truth. And then I want you to get me away from them as quickly as possible, and I never want to go back, Tim. Never," she stated.

He reached over and with love and tenderness he massaged her cold hands. "Calm down, baby. See, this is why I didn't want you to go to Memphis. I don't like seeing you like this. It's not good for you. I want your life to be as stress free as possible."

"I know you do, and so do I. But I have to do this. I have to get this behind me once and for all." Francesca picked up her cell phone from the console and started twiddling it between her fingers. She looked at the clock on the dash. "We should be there in, what? About another twenty minutes, or so?"

"Yeah, that last sign said we had twenty-five miles to go. And we're already on the outskirts. I say we should make it to your father's apartment in about thirty, no later than forty minutes."

Francesca exhaled. "I'm glad Jackson is only a short distance from Memphis."

"Are you getting ready to call him?" Tim eyed the phone she held briefly before focusing back on the road.

"No, I told you that I don't have his number."

"Oh, yeah, that's right. My bad. I forgot."

"It doesn't matter because we're going to stay in Memphis until I see him. I don't care if we have to wait all night."

Francesca's voice sounded harsh. She sounded like the old Francesca. The Francesca that used to rule the women she messed around with. The Francesca that had her female lovers cowering when she got angry. She used to have a bad temper and there were times in her past that she didn't hesitate to let it loose. She would strike without warning. Rena could attest to that. But since she'd repented and recommitted her life to God, with His help she had been able to maintain self-control. Plus, Tim wasn't the type of person who brought out that wicked side of her. Tim was gentle, kind, understanding and patient. He had an easy going personality and was very non-argumentative. He had a way of keeping her calm and composed. Like now, Tim recognized she was becoming agitated so this time he burst out singing with the radio when he heard the tune by Tyrese. *"Ooh baby, be my sweet lady..."*

Francesca couldn't help it. She looked at Tim and burst out laughing. "Okay, okay, I promise to stop stressing if you promise to stop singing," she said between bouts of laughter. "You are messing up Tyrese's song."

"Me? How can you hurt my feelings like that?" he joked. "You are my sweet lady. I can't believe you'd rather listen to him," he said pointing at the radio, "rather than me. Check it out" and he started singing along with the radio again. *"I'll be there if you need me, you can call or believe me."*

She lightly tapped him on his thigh. “See, you don’t even know the words.” She laughed even louder this time. “You need to stick to your white boy songs or something. Don’t be going around messing up our songs.”

“Oh, so now we’re a little racist. How can you be racist against your own husband?” Tim enjoyed seeing Francesca laugh. She had a way of brightening up a room with her laugher.

“Whateva,” she replied. “You can call it what you want, but you are not a soul singer. I love you and all, but please, stick to your day job.”

“Okay, if you insist,” he said. “But you’re still racist.”

“Yeah, right. But I only have eyes for you, white boy. Only you.”

“And let’s keep it like that.” He smiled.

They turned into pastor’s neighborhood.

Tim made several more turns before he arrived at Pastor’s apartment complex. He followed the car in front of him when the gate opened and made it inside the complex before the gate closed back. Pulling into an empty space, he turned off the ignition and then focused all of his attention on Francesca.

“What?” She looked at him looking at her. “Why are you staring at me like that?” She reached for her door handle but Tim stopped her from getting out the car by holding on to her elbow.

“Look, there’s one thing I want to ask you to do?”

“What’s that?” she said.

“Listen to everything he has to say before you go off or jump to your own conclusions. Like I said, I do not, and I mean do not want you getting yourself all upset. We know what Stiles said and all you’re here to do is listen to what your father has to say about it all. Okay?”

Francesca was quiet momentarily like she was pondering Tim's words in her mind. "I promise. Now, can we go in?"

Tim nodded. They walked along the walkway toward Pastor's apartment. Tim knocked on the door.

Pastor answered the door within seconds. "Well I'll be. Isn't this a pleasant surprise," he said and invited Francesca and Tim inside.

He tried to kiss Francesca when she walked into the apartment but she leaned back to avoid him. He didn't say a word. Instead he focused his attention on Tim.

"Hello, Tim. How are you?"

"If I don't consider the fact that the latest round of drama in the Graham household has stressed out my wife, then I'd say I'm good. But we both know that's not the case."

Pastor cleared his throat. He looked uncomfortable. "Come on in the living room. Can I get y'all something to eat?" He looked at his daughter. "Drink?

"I'm fine," she said.

"So am I," Tim answered.

"How long y'all been in Memphis?" Pastor sounded more like he was probing.

"Just long enough to be sitting here. Pastor, how could you? Why did you do it?" Francesca quickly lit in on him after they had barely taken their seats.

"I don't know what all Stiles told you, but I did what I thought was best at the time. That's all we can do, honey. As a child of God, I prayed hard about my decision and my advice to your mother. Audrey was the core of my life and you know that, so I would never do anything that I thought would hurt her."

Francesca started twisting her hands together, an obvious sign of her mounting frustration with all that had transpired over the last few weeks. She was fed up with her family's secrets and the way they went about doing things. It was like there was always something they were hiding and then they always wanted to justify their actions by putting God in the midst of their mess.

"But obviously your advice didn't help now, did it, Pastor? I mean your wife hated me. And really, I can't say I blame her. I mean, if I had been attacked and raped, gotten pregnant by my rapist and then made to keep the child, I would probably have been just like her. I would hate me too. But that's what you did. You were the reason for this."

"But you're here. Yes, she could have aborted you and then we wouldn't be sitting across from each other right now. Francesca, please try to understand. I know your mother had a tough time dealing with the decision she made, but she made it. And, you should know your mother. If she really didn't want to keep you, there's no way she would have. Once that woman made up her mind about something, nobody, not even me could make her change it. So, I won't take full responsibility for it. And I'm not sorry about it either. I love you. You're my daughter."

"No, that's where you're wrong," Francesca suddenly yelled. "I'm not your daughter. And you're not my father. You're just a bully dressed all up in your God clothes. All the while you forced her to do something she didn't want to do. You forced her to carry me in her belly for nine months."

Tim reached out to console his wife but Francesca jumped up off the sofa before he could grab hold of her.

She got up and walked over to Pastor who was seated in his recliner. "You're a fake, a hypocrite. You and Stiles are cut from the same cloth. You're nothing but wannabes. Always want folks to think you're so high and mighty. But I see right through your mess. And..."

It was Pastor's turn to stand up and he did as quickly as his legs could move. "Don't you talk to me like that, young lady. Don't you ever talk to me like that. I know who I believe. I am a God fearing man. You want to blame all of your mistakes on me? Well, I won't have it anymore."

"You won't have it? Oh, see that's the problem right there, you never took ownership of anything. You're a coward."

Tim jumped up and grabbed hold of Francesca as she spat venom at Pastor over and over again until Tim could see him start to tremble.

"Calm down, Francesca. You're upsetting him."

She turned toward Tim and gave him such a mean look that if looks could kill he would have been dead on the spot. "I know you aren't taking up for this, this...bully."

"I've had enough," Pastor screamed. "I'm tired of you always blaming somebody else for the mess you made of your life. You're just like your mother." Spittle flew from Pastor's mouth as he spoke. His voice became louder and his mounting anger was obvious.

"You want to know the truth? You want to hear the real truth? Then I'll give you the real truth. Your mother was wild and untamed just like you," he screamed. "I tried to make her into something she wasn't. She loved the streets. She loved to party. I knew that when I met her. But I had prayed for a woman, and when she came into my life and with your brother too, I fell for her. She was a stunner. Beautiful, knew all the right words to say."

"Oh, so now you're going to make this out to be her fault?" Francesca started chuckling uncontrollably. "You're really something else. Audrey may have been a lot of things, and she may have been wild and untamed, so you say, but that doesn't mean she deserved to be raped. It doesn't mean she should have been forced to have a baby that she didn't want. I really see the real you for the first time in my life.

I should have seen it a long time ago. All wrapped up in the church but neglecting your wife. It's your fault she was raped. If you had been home with her instead of spending all your time at Holy Rock, maybe none of this would have happened. Just like you're the reason I was raped and molested. You," she kept screaming and pointing a finger all up in Pastor's face.

"I'm sorry to tell you this, but tour mother was no saint, Francesca. And the truth is she wasn't raped," he yelled out suddenly, seemingly stunning himself with the words that shot forth from his mouth.

"What did you say?" Francesca asked.

"I said, Audrey was never raped," Pastor repeated but this time in a milder tone.

"What do you mean she wasn't raped? Now you're going to tell me she asked for it? Is that what you're trying to say? Why you, low down, evil..."

"She had an affair," he screamed at Francesca. "She wasn't raped. Maybe I could have taken it better if she had been. Lord forgive me for saying that, but it's true. Your mother was having an affair with one of the neighbors. I had suspected it, suspected it for a long time, but I just didn't want to face it." Pastor's face turned crimson and his voice began to sound deflated but he kept talking like he couldn't control himself.

"I guess I thought if I ignored it, that it would just dissolve by itself, go away. Me and her, we wanted a baby of our own, and we would have had one I'm sure of it, if she hadn't messed off with Jerry."

Francesca almost fell backward but Tim was holding her steady.

"And me, I guess you could call me just plain stupid. When she told me she was pregnant, I believed it was mine. I wanted it to be mine, and she let me believe it until the day I caught her and Jerry together, in my house and in my bed. I wanted to kill her and him. God knows I hated her at that moment. Me and him got into a big fight and I beat him down. She was screaming and yelling, pleading for me to stop.

"Turns out the joke was on me, because after I bloodied him up real good, she turned on me, told me she was pregnant with his child. She was furious at me for confronting the guy the way I did. She started ranting and spewing all kinds of obscenities at me, can you believe that?" he asked but not waiting on a response from Francesca.

"Only problem with that, Jerry already had a wife. Three kids too. He had no plans to leave Connie and his children. And he told Audrey that. Told her right in front of me. Told her to have an abortion, do whatever but he wasn't going to mess up his family for her.

"You're lying," Francesca accused him.

"I wish I was, but I'm not. That night, she left us both standing in the middle of our bedroom. Jerry with a bloody, broken nose, and me with a broken heart. I didn't see or hear from her for over a week. When she did come back home, I had already made up in my mind that I was going to forgive her. I had to. I mean,

God forgives us over and over again. Who was I not to do the same?"

Francesca continued to stare at Pastor. "So now you want me to believe you were some self-righteous, perfect, never made a mistake saint? Puhleeze, you sicken me. And Audrey," Francesca chuckled loudly, "She was definitely a piece of work. Running the church and the streets at the same time." She kept laughing hysterically.

It was apparent that neither of them, including Tim heard Stiles when he came into the apartment.

"You're lying," Stiles yelled. Francesca abruptly stopped laughing. They all looked toward the sound of his voice. "You're trying to save your own hide by feeding these lies to her?" he pointed at Francesca and frowned like he was disgusted by the sight of her. He pursed his lips together and took two steps toward Pastor. Tim released Francesca and jumped into the space separating Pastor and Stiles. He didn't know if Stiles was about to strike Pastor or not. But he wasn't going to take any chances.

"Stop it. Everybody," Tim yelled. "This is nonsense. Get it together. Y'all are all out of control."

"I'm tired of being silent about everything," Pastor said. "The bottom line remains whether you like it or not, your mother did what she did and I did what I thought was therapeutic for her. Maybe she felt like she had been raped after Jerry walked out on her. I don't know. I can't say why she wrote those lies, only God knows.

"Audrey had her own way of dealing with her mistakes. But one thing is true, I didn't want her to have an abortion because there was a chance the baby she was carrying was mine. I couldn't let her go through with it. But she was set on having one anyway. Said she knew it was Jerry's and if she couldn't have him, she didn't want any parts of him. But ends up she was too far along and no doctor would perform the abortion. So for the next few months, I lived in turmoil.

"Pardon my French, but your mother was *hell* to live with. She cried for days and weeks at a time after that. Jerry moved his family to God knows where. I haven't seen or heard from him since. May have moved out of town for all I know. But Audrey took it hard, real hard. She even had a difficult, real difficult labor. Wouldn't let me be in the room with her or nothing," he said. "Right after you were born she demanded a DNA test. I didn't want one. Plus she wouldn't be able to test Jerry. And I was going to love you no matter what."

"Ohhh, how gallant and noble of you," Francesca said with bitter sarcasm.

Tim stepped back to his wife's side and wrapped his arms around her waist.

"So, what are you saying? What other lies are you getting ready to spill now?" Stiles butt in.

Pastor looked over at Francesca with saddened eyes, ignoring what Stiles said. "Your mother was right."

"You're lying. If you weren't an old man, I'd kick your butt from here to kingdom come," Stiles threatened. "You're pathetic. You wait until my poor mother is dead in her grave and you want to disgrace her name now. What? You think this is going to make you look good? Think Francesca is going to love you now?" Stiles chuckled with a wickedness that penetrated the already volatile atmosphere.

"No matter what the circumstances, the fact remains," Francesca said softly, "she hated me. I might as well have been the child of a rapist. At least I would have understood why she hated me so much. But she hated me because the man she loved didn't love her in return and she was forced to keep his child. A baby he walked out on."

"I'm sorry, darling," Pastor managed to say as tears flowed down his ever wrinkling cheeks. "I didn't want you to find out like this. I didn't want you to find out at all, but I didn't know she had written that letter. She never gave it to me. And I don't know why she said what she said. Maybe she felt like she *had* been raped and violated. Who knows what was going on through her head back then. But we worked it out. She became fiercely loyal and loving toward me, and soon the past was forgotten and we went on to have a wonderful marriage. There were times we hoped she would get pregnant again, but she didn't. God only knows why she kept those news clippings. Your mother, she always made sure she had a ram in the bush."

"Stop it. You're hiding behind my mother's death," Stiles said with force. "You know she's not here to defend herself, so you're making up all these lies to make yourself look good. If the folks at Holy Rock could hear you now. I hope you rot in hell for what you've done to this family."

"Get me out of here," Francesca ordered Tim. "I'm going to be sick," she said and started gagging. Tim scooped her up and carried her to Pastor's bathroom. When the two of them came back to the living room, Stiles was gone and Pastor was seated in his recliner with his head in his hands.

Francesca slowly walked past him with Tim holding on to her.

Tim turned. “I’m going to pray for you. It’s all I can do,” he told Pastor as they walked out of Pastor’s apartment leaving the door open behind them.

20

"A pure hand needs no glove to cover it." - The Scarlet Letter

Stiles had been at Holy Rock most of the morning, and so Detria took a chance and did something she'd never done before; she invited Skip to come to the house for a quick rump in the same bed she and Stiles shared.

She had promised God that she wouldn't sleep with him again, but she was too weak resist Skip Madison. There was just something about him, something that drew her under like a curse or a spell.

She had just finished her bath and putting the soiled linen in the washer when she heard Stiles enter the house with a bang. She jumped. He had slammed the door with what sounded like full force. She rushed into the kitchen to see what was going on.

"What's wrong with you?" Detria asked after she saw the look on Stiles's face as he entered the house. "You look like you just witnessed a murder or something."

He paced back and forth across the hardwood floors of their family room while Baby Audrey sat on a throw in the floor playing with toys.

"I'm just. I don't know what I am, Detria. I don't know what to do. I don't know what to believe. God, help me," he said before he went to his favorite chair and sat down.

"Stiles, please, you're scaring me. What's wrong with you."

Detria quickly dismissed the thoughts she was having about her earlier tryst with Skip. For a second she thought Stiles had run into Skip leaving their house, but then she realized that couldn't have been possible because Skip had been gone for at least thirty minutes.

"Detria," he was shaking his head from side to side as he came near her.

"Tell me, what's wrong? You're scaring the baby too. Look how she's looking at you," Detria said, looking over at her daughter. "She's getting ready to cry."

"I know. I'm sorry." Stiles got up and walked over to Baby Audrey, squatted down next to her and started playing with her. For the next few minutes he entertained her, while toying over in his mind the events that had transpired earlier. *How much more was being hidden? Was Pastor really telling the truth about Audrey? Where did the truth end and the lies begin?* These were questions he tossed over and over again in his mind.

"Baby, did something happen at church? Did somebody die?"

Stiles always took it hard when one of his members went to be with the Lord. Folks at the church didn't witness that side of Stiles, but Detria often witnessed his hurt first hand. He would sometimes go into his study and cry and pray for hours after funeralizing one of their church members, especially those who he had come to know on a more personal level. It was hard for Detria to watch him, to see him during those times of despair. Most people seemed not to realize that pastors grieve too. Detria hadn't thought much about it herself until she became Stiles' wife.

"No, everything's all right at the church. It's Pastor. Pastor, Audrey, Francesca, everybody." He stuck a toy in one of Baby Audrey's hands and stood upright while rubbing his own hand back and forth on the crown of his head.

"What about them? What's going on, Stiles? You look like you've seen a ghost."

Stiles walked over to the nearby king-sized ottoman and sat on its edge. He told Detria everything that had happened. When he finished, Detria's hand covered her open mouth.

"Are you serious? I can't believe this. What was Pastor thinking? I don't know why he would tell y'all something like that anyway."

Stiles looked at her. "What do you mean by that? I guess the man finally realized that it was time for him to cough up the truth. It's so unbelievable though. It's left me more confused than ever. I don't know what to believe."

"Well, seems to me there's no reason for him to lie about it. I mean, all lying is going to do is make things that much worse." Detria paused. "That is, if things could get any worse. And poor Francesca. I know she must have taken it hard. That woman has been through so much. I don't know how she does it."

"It's not just Francesca," Stiles said in a biting tone and cut his eyes at his wife. "I've been hurt by this whole thing and then on top of all at that, my poor dead mother's name has been ruined. How could he do that? As much as she loved that man and he sits up and tells us that she had an affair on him. It just doesn't make sense for her to lie like that. And what about the newspaper clippings. Why did she have them? None of it makes sense."

Detria shifted nervously in her seat. A wave of guilt came over her as she listened to Stiles talk about Audrey's affair with another man. But things were different, or maybe they weren't. She heard Stiles talking but she couldn't for the life of her understand what he was saying. *Skip, you wouldn't walk out on me. You wouldn't do me like that man did Audrey would you. What we have, well it's different, and I'm in control of the situation anyway. I wouldn't fall weak to you like it's obvious that Audrey did. Stupid woman.*

"I'm sorry, honey. Maybe your mother found it easier to cope with the thought of being raped than to face the fact that her husband caught her with her lover. The same lover who turned around and walked out on her. I really don't know," Detria said sounding just as confused as Stiles.

"But, look why don't I make us something to eat. And while I'm doing that your daughter can keep you company. That way your mind won't be occupied with worrying about Pastor and his confessions. It's a crying shame the way that man has done you and Francesca. And he's supposed to be so righteous and upright. I tell you, it's those kind of—"

Stiles put up a show of hands. “Stop it, Detria. Just stop it. I don’t want to hear it.” He pounced up like a panther from off the ottoman. “I’m not hungry,” he said and stormed out of the family room.

Detria heard him as he pounced up the stairs. Suit yourself. “I was just trying to be nice,” she mumbled. Baby Audrey started crying. “Stiles,” Detria called. “Stiles, the baby’s crying.”

Stiles didn’t respond nor did he come back downstairs.

“Dang,” she said and walked over to where Baby Audrey was flailing her arms and going into one of her temper tantrums. The baby hated to be left alone. She loved to have someone up in her face all the time. “You’re just like your grandmother. You always want the spotlight on you,” she said to the baby as she grabbed her off the floor and placed her on her hip. “Be quiet,” she said in an elevated voice. “I’m not for all this crying.”

She walked into the kitchen and went over to the refrigerator. She removed an orange sippy cup and closed the door to the stainless steel appliance. “Here,” she said and gave Baby Audrey the sippy cup full of apple juice. “Now shut your mouth and drink this. You’re sleepy anyway.”

Detria returned to the family room and pulled out Audrey’s portable crib and placed the child in it before she turned and walked off and went back into the kitchen. “I’ll be right back. I’m just going to go in here and fix me a sandwich. So don’t start all that crying again. I mean it too.”

Detria made herself a turkey sandwich with the fixings and a glass of iced tea, and then returned to where Baby Audrey was sitting in her crib, nodding. She was barely holding on to her sippy cup. The scene would have made for an adorable picture but Detria wasn't the picture taking type. She sat her food on the nearby table and then walked over to the crib to lay Baby Audrey down.

Baby Audrey started crying again. "I told you I wasn't going to have all this noise. Shut up and drink that juice and go to sleep," she ordered the infant who seemed to understand her mother because instantly she became quiet, put the sippy cup in her mouth, and closed her eyes

Detria took a couple of bites of her sandwich and then retrieved her cell phone from the same table where she'd set her food.

She listened to the phone ring. The voice mail came on. "Hi, this is Skip. Sorry I'm unavailable to take your call, but if you leave a message I'll get back to you as soon as I can."

"Hey, babe. It's me. I'm still thinking about our little meet and greet earlier. That was fun." She laughed into the phone. "Anyway, call me when you can. You are not going to believe what I have to tell you."

◊

Francesca cried almost all the way to Jackson. Tim was furious. The Graham family was looney tunes in his book. How could they go around destroying each other's lives over and over again? Didn't they practice what they preached? It was becoming more apparent to Tim that they didn't or else his wife wouldn't be sitting across from him distraught.

"Francesca, please, baby. Please don't cry. It's going to be all right. I promise you it will. You don't ever have to go back there again. You don't ever have to see them or talk to them again if you don't want to."

"I just want to be at home. I want to go home, Tim. Please, just get me home," she pleaded tearfully.

"I am, honey. Just hold tight. And stop crying. You're going to make yourself sick. And you know we don't want that. The enemy is just trying to mess with your head, and we aren't going to let him do that. We've got too many positive things going for us." He reached over and massaged her shoulder with his free hand.

"I love you, Francesca. I love you so much," he said in a soothing voice. "Shhh, it's going to be all right."

Francesca began to calm down but her breathing remained heavy. "It's not fair, Tim." She shook her head. "It's not fair."

"I know it isn't, but God is still a just God. He knows your pain and he's got your back. You have to believe that. You have to trust Him, baby."

She sniffled a few times before she answered. "I know, but I still wish I knew the purpose for all of this, for everything I'm going through. I just don't understand any of it, Tim. I swear I don't."

"Shhh, don't swear. Just trust Him. He says we shouldn't lean to our own understanding. His ways are not our ways and his—"

"His thoughts are not our thoughts," she finished. "But it still doesn't make me feel any better. I feel like my heart is about to burst wide open. Those folks act like they *want* to see me dead."

"Well, those folks," Tim repeated, "are not going to get the satisfaction. Believe that."

Francesca looked at her husband. "You're a Godsend. I don't know how I would have made it this far without you."

Tim smiled and quickly leaned over and pecked her on the cheek.

◊

Sister Josie walked into the apartment to a stoic and quiet Pastor. "What's wrong? I saw Stiles and what looked like your daughter leaving a few minutes ago. Is everything all right over here?"

Pastor nodded.

"Chauncey, I know you. And you don't look right. What is it?" she asked.

"Nothing. Everything's fine. The kids and I had some things we had to clear up. Everything is done and over with. Nothing for you to worry about."

"Well, I am worried because you don't look right. Is your daughter okay?"

"Josie, it's nothing. Believe me. Everything is fine."

Pastor didn't mean to tell them about Audrey's affair, but the words spewed out before he could stop them. With Francesca down his throat and pounding him with one question after another, he couldn't keep up the web of deceit any longer. He'd lived with the secrets of Audrey's indiscretions for far too long. He hated that Francesca and Stiles had to find out the way that they did, but the lies were too much. He loved his wife, loved her for over thirty years, but it had never been enough for Audrey.

When he walked in on her and Jerry in his own house that day, he wanted to commit murder. It was only by the grace and mercy of God that he didn't. Instead he and Jerry had fought fist to fist with Audrey screaming and yelling for them to stop. Actually for him to stop pounding the life out of Jerry. Pastor's anger had produced a crazed like maniac and a hulk like strength took over. The only thing that stopped him from killing Jerry back then was Audrey. When she hollered that she was pregnant, it threw him into shock and his hands seemed to stop in mid-air.

Audrey didn't hide her feelings back then. She made it clear that it was Jerry she loved, Jerry she wanted to be with. She wanted to have his love child. But Jerry didn't want anything to do with her or the child she was carrying. But it was too late for Audrey. She was forced to go through the pregnancy because she was too far along in her pregnancy to have an abortion.

The pregnancy was harsh on Audrey and even the labor was long. Pastor tried to support her while he was going through his own personal torment. He had no one to turn to, so he endured the pain of his wife's blatant infidelity in silence. Knowing full well that she was carrying another man's baby almost killed him.

Audrey was to blame for the decisions she'd made back then, and from the time Francesca entered the world, she had raised her at a distance. She never really bore an attachment to the child.

Pastor wanted to ignore the truth, tried hard to ignore the truth, and he succeeded to a point by keeping busy with whatever was going on at Holy Rock. As time passed, he immersed himself more and more into church business, and spent as much time as he could building up the church while his family structure slowly crumbled.

"I'm going back home. I see you're not in the mood for company."

Pastor looked up like he was just stepping into the room. "I'm sorry, Josie. I guess my mind drifted off for a moment. You don't have to go."

"No, I just came over to make sure you were okay. You hadn't said anything about your daughter coming to town, so I was just concerned when I saw her and Stiles."

"Thanks for caring about me," he said, his voice fading away.

Josie brushed her lips against his. "I'll be back in time for Judge Judy," she said and then turned to leave. "And don't bother getting up, I'll lock the door behind me."

"Thanks, Josie. I'll see you in a couple of hours."

Pastor went to his bedroom, and sat in the chair next to the window. From his bedroom chair, he could see the family of birds and squirrels that had claimed the massive oak tree as their home. He stared outside, and began to reminisce about how he had fallen in love with Audrey almost instantly. The day she strolled into Holy Rock was forever etched in his mind and stamped on his heart. It was that deep, abiding love that he had for her that made him forgive her. Adding insult to injury, when tests proved that he was not Francesca's biological father, it was another blow he took to his heart, but yet again he couldn't see himself being parted from his dear beloved Audrey.

◊

Upstairs in his study, Stiles tried to drown out everything that had happened out of his mind. He turned on his IPod and the music blasted from the iPod speakers. The first song that came on was "For Every Mountain" one of the songs on Sunday Best Winner Amber Bullock's debut album. *I've got so much to thank God for. So many wonderful blessings...*

Stiles didn't want to admit it, didn't want to think it, but somehow the human part of him, the man part of him, the fleshly part of him, questioned how he could give God praise when all around his world was crumbling.

21

"All discarded lovers should be given a second chance, but with somebody else." Mae West

Rena was thrilled about the way her life was unfolding. Her marriage to Robert was picture perfect. They had recently found out through an ultrasound that Rena was not carrying one baby, but two. She couldn't believe that she was actually carrying twins. Twin girls at that. It was a welcoming surprise.

Her first trimester had been fairly easy, and now she was going into her second without any complications. She'd been following doctor's orders to the letter, being careful to heed to everything that would increase the chances of giving birth to two healthy babies.

She'd experienced only one outbreak since the pregnancy. It had been troubling to Rena at first, but Robert tried to convince her that the babies would be just fine. Right away, she called and made an appointment with her OB/GYN. She was not about to do anything that would compromise the health of her babies.

"Mrs. Becton, I understand your concern about transmitting the disease to your babies, but I told you, please don't worry," the doctor stated. "I need you to take care of yourself during this pregnancy. You're carrying twins, and that's enough added pressure, strain and stress on you.

Remember that I told you that it is rare for expecting mothers who have recurrent genital herpes to transmit it to their babies. I'm not saying that it's one hundred percent, but I'm saying it's rare. And also," the doctor said, "because you've had the disease for some time now, you have a natural protection formed from antibodies," she patiently explained to Rena once again. "Those antibodies are in your bloodstream. They connect with the placenta and move on to the fetus which in turn helps to protect your babies from the disease. So, please, let your body do what it was designed to do. Okay?"

Rena nodded and so did Robert. He put his arm around her shoulder.

"Stress and worry isn't good for you, or the babies. Period."

"That's what I keep telling her, doc," Robert interjected.

"Listen to your husband, Mrs. Becton. Stress and worry can also increase the chance of outbreaks. Your body is going through a lot right now. So much happens when a woman becomes pregnant. But you can do this, Mrs. Becton. You can make it through this. And I'm with you all the way." The doctor turned and looked at

Robert. “And,” she looked at Robert, “Mr. Becton, whatever you can do to keep her calm, please do it.”

“Oh, most definitely. I told her that everything would be fine. She just has to have faith.”

“See, listen to this man,” the doctor said and laughed. “We’re watching you closely throughout this pregnancy. There are so many expectant mothers who don’t even know they have the disease. Those are the ones we’re really concerned about because they stand a chance of delivering a baby with neonatal herpes. But you, you’re educated about the disease. You know what to look for. That’s a huge plus for you and for your babies. So, please, if you do have another outbreak, I want you to call just like you did this time, and make an appointment. Okay?”

Rena nodded again and Robert held onto her hand as they both listened.

“You feel better, honey?” Robert asked when they left the doctor’s office.

“Yes, I guess. I just want our babies to be okay, Robert. I don’t want them to suffer because of my mistakes. God, I pray that they don’t.”

Robert started the car, but before he put it in gear he turned toward Rena. “They’re going to be fine. You’ll see. Our twin girls are going to be not only beautiful, but one hundred percent perfect in every way.” He smiled at Rena then kissed her on her lips.

She welcomed his soft lips on hers and instantly she began to feel relaxed.

◊

Robert and Rena had been talking to a lawyer about Rena adopting his kids. Robert hadn’t seen or heard from Isabelle and Robbie's mother for almost three years. No one knew where she was or how she was doing, including her family. Rena hoped and prayed that the adoptions would go through.

She no longer gave a thought about Francesca or Stiles either for that matter. The condom incident was long pushed aside. She did finally tell Robert about it because this time she didn't want to risk anything bad happening in her marriage. He told her to let it go, let the past remain in the past and move forward; that there was always going to be somebody who hates on another person.

Rena was endeared to Robert even more after that. Once again, he had displayed another part of him that reassured her that she had chosen the right guy.

She couldn't understand why Francesca or Stiles would hate on her. She'd done nothing but love them. She loved Francesca in her own way and she was in love with Stiles. True, she had deceived him, but it wasn't meant to hurt him. She didn't tell him about the relationship between her and Frankie because she wanted to protect him, and plus she was ashamed of how she allowed her and Frankie's relationship to get out of hand for so long. But now she had finally come to grips with her past. She'd forgiven herself the way God had done so very long ago. Rena could actually smile from the inside out.

She massaged her round growing belly and giggled when one of the babies kicked.

"Robert," she hurried into his man cave. "One of the twins just kicked me. Feel right here," she told him as she walked up on him. He looked away from the game that was playing on ESPN and gave his undivided attention to his wife.

Rena took hold of his hand and placed it on the spot where the baby kicked. Robert jumped when the baby kicked against his hand.

His laughter seemed to fill the air. The kids came running into the family room. "Come here, Isabelle. You too, Robbie," Robert told them. They ran up and stood next to their father. "Here, feel this." He took each of their hands and placed them on Rena's swollen belly. "Now you have to be real quiet and still," he said in a doting voice.

Robbie was the first to laugh. "It moved, mommy," he said to Rena. He had been calling her mommy for close to two years. At first Isabelle called her Aunty Rena but followed suit shortly after Robbie started calling her 'mommy'.

"No it didn't," Isabelle countered. "I didn't feel nothing."

"I didn't feel anything," Robert corrected.

"Hold on, give them a second. You'll feel them kicking. Well, at least one of them," Rena assured Isabelle. "Come on, put your hand right here." This time Rena guided her hand. Isabelle placed her head against Rena's belly too. Suddenly her head popped up and a big toothless grin spilled across her face.

"I felt her. I felt the baby," she squealed with delight. The four of them became consumed with touching Rena's belly. All was good in the Becton household.

◇

Isabelle and Robbie were asleep in their rooms. Robert pulled Rena next to him. His warm, passionate kisses covered her like a blanket.

"Baby, I'm so happy," she managed to say as he gently caressed her. "I'm so happy."

A flashback flooded her mind and she saw Stiles kissing her, and then just as quickly Robert's face turned to the likeness of Frankie. What was going on? She shook her head.

"What is it?" Robert stopped midstream.

"Uh, nothing. It's nothing."

"Are the babies all right? Do you want to do this?"

"They're fine. And yes, I want to do this," she answered.

Rena looked at him with adoring eyes. Robert was so considerate and so thoughtful. He was always putting her needs or the needs of the kids before his own. He was definitely her knight in shiny armor, and every day she thanked God for giving her a second chance. A second chance at love.

"Honey, I'm fine," she reassured her husband. This time she became the aggressor. She pushed thoughts of Stiles and Frankie out of her mind and snuggled against him, intertwining her legs with his. Her body melted against his and skin to skin they became one.

22

"Every tomorrow has two handles. We can take hold of it with the handle of anxiety or the handle of faith." Henry Ward Beecher

The next several months passed by in a blur. Francesca had refused Pastor's and Stiles' calls. At first they would called almost every day, sometimes two or three times a day after she'd left Memphis. Even Detria called and left a few messages but Francesca didn't respond to her either. She wanted nothing more to do with her family. After all, she wasn't really a part of their family anyway.

This man named Jerry that Pastor talked about never wanted her, her mother didn't want her, and Pastor, well in Francesca's eyes he only kept her because it was too late for Audrey to do away with her, and he probably wanted to save face at the church.

The more she thought about everything, the more she started to become more relaxed. *One*, because she felt a sense of freedom in a way. Not truly being connected to the Graham family was her way out.

Two, sure, Stiles may have been her brother, but their relationship was totally severed now. Plus, he was too much like Audrey, and Francesca recognized that even more when she was in Memphis. Everybody thought he was a Mr. Goody Two Shoes, but Francesca was well aware of his darker side. Rena should have seen it for herself when he kicked her to the curb. And Detria, well, Francesca had a feeling that Detria had tasted a bit of Stiles' venom too whether she would admit it or not.

Francesca couldn't quite put a finger on why she felt that way about Detria, but there was something in Detria's mannerisms and the times they used to talk on the phone, that caused Francesca to suspect that Stiles had shown his true colors a time or two.

As for Pastor, now that she knew he wasn't her real father she didn't feel like she owed him a thing. If anything, she'd given him a way out. He wouldn't have to put on a sham any longer, pretending like he loved and cared about her so much. No wonder he didn't stand up like a real father would have done after knowing his daughter, his only daughter at that had been molested and raped. He knew all along that she wasn't his, and Francesca believed that no matter how he may have wanted to feel true love for her as his own, he could not. She was another man's child. A man Pastor knew. His neighbor. A man who betrayed him by coming into his home, his sanctuary and bedding his wife.

And Audrey, well she still managed to have the last laugh it seemed. Even from her grave, she still held the trump card. What was the reason she left those newspaper clippings and that fake letter? Francesca toiled over it again and again. The only thing she could come up with was that Audrey always had to be the victim. She could never be the one to let sleeping dogs lie as the old folks used to say. If she wasn't stirring up mess, then she wouldn't be Audrey Graham. So even from her grave, she managed to wreak havoc. How could she say she loved anybody? How could Audrey even say that she loved Pastor when she could leave behind a letter riddled with lies? And Pastor, he had to be plain naïve or stupid. Francesca hadn't decided which category he fit in best.

Tim told her that one day she was going to have to find it in her heart to forgive her family. It was the only way she could be forgiven, he told her. She believed that she could forgive Pastor, Stiles, Audrey and all the people who had wronged her in life, but she didn't have to forget what they'd done. Maybe that wasn't how God operated, but Francesca wasn't God, she was a woman who had been hurt, whose spirit had been crushed by those who pretended to love her.

These last few weeks she told herself that Stiles and Pastor must have finally gotten the message that she didn't want anything to do with them because the calls had stopped. Slowly, she got back into her routine of taking care of her health, her spirit, and her man.

"Tim, I can't wait until tomorrow," Francesca said with her legs propped up on his thighs.

"Me neither," he said as they sat in their family room with a bowl of air popped popcorn on the table in front of them. They were posted in front of the giant flat screen TV mounted on the wall, and Tim flipped through the Netflix catalog of movies.

"Do you think they're going to finally approve us to adopt a child?" asked Francesca.

"With God all things are possible."

"Uh oh. That means you think they aren't. I know I have AIDS but that doesn't mean I can pass it on to a child. They shouldn't be able to deny us because of it either. People need to be more educated about AIDS."

"People *are* more educated," Tim said, "but it doesn't mean that we won't go through a lot of red tape to get approved for adoption. Shucks, people who are perfectly healthy, squeaky clean and all, have a hard time. And really, I don't blame the adoption agencies. They have to be sure they pair these children up with good parents. Think about that woman who adopted that little boy from over in Russia and then when he didn't measure up to her misconstrued, twisted ideals of what a child should be she shipped him back with a tag pinned on his clothes."

"What? I didn't hear about that? When did that happen?"

"A few years ago."

"That's awful. But we're not like that. We have a lot of love to give to a child. You know it and I know it."

"Yes, we do, and that's why I'm not going to worry about a thing. God knows our hearts, and He knows the desires of our heart. And because of that, I believe that everything is going to work out as it should."

"You're right. You're always right," Francesca told him and cuddled up even closer to him. They settled on a thriller movie to watch. They both loved a good thriller. Francesca reached for the bowl of popcorn, placed it on top of them, and they settled back as the movie began.

23

"The worst way to miss someone is when they are right beside you and yet you know you can never have them." Unknown

Detria sat behind the desk in her office at Holy Rock reminiscing about the earlier rendezvous she'd had with Skip. She'd left the hotel an hour earlier and he was going to stop by his house, change clothes and come to the church. They'd decided to stop meeting at his house. It was too risky so they'd made one of the hotels out in the suburbs their new meeting place.

Detria tried to concentrate on the paperwork before her. She was actually proud of the job she'd done with the children's ministry. It was rapidly expanding under her leadership. It wasn't that she adored kids so much; well she actually really did like kids as long as they weren't hers.

She figured she couldn't love Baby Audrey as much as she wanted to because she didn't love her 'baby daddy' as much as she hoped she would when she married him. She told herself she could love him easily. After all, Stiles was supposed to have been a good catch by her parents' definition. He was a Godly man, a handsome man, a great provider and he treated her well. He was fairly good in bed, yet Detria felt like there was always something missing in their marriage. It was like Stiles never could quite give all of himself to her, and she sensed it.

Rena may have married Robert Becton, who Detria perceived to be a decent guy, but one that Rena probably didn't truly love either. Detria believed that Rena still had feelings for her husband. At first, it used to hurt to know that her husband probably was still in love with his ex-wife.

Too bad things didn't blow up when Detria sent those condoms to Rena. Detria couldn't figure out what happened with that. Stiles hadn't said anything to her about it, and Rena as far as Detria knew had never contacted Stiles. But then again, who knows, maybe they had talked. Detria didn't trust either one of them.

Enter Skip. Detria hadn't meant for them to hook up. But, as people say, things happen and she was a young, vibrant woman with needs. Needs that her husband was too busy to attend to because he was always at Holy Rock or on campus teaching.

She couldn't help it if Skip and Stiles were good friends. And it wasn't her fault that her husband didn't touch her as often as she wanted him to, needed him to.

Things had started off so innocently between her and Skip. A smile here. A kind word there. An extra minute or two of conversation.

Detria couldn't pinpoint when like for Skip had turned to lust, but ever since it did, there had been no turning back. She sat at her desk and daydreamed about their time together. They'd spent half of the morning in bed making love.

"Detria, we've been together for a while, and keeping this thing between us a secret is getting harder every day," Skip said as he cradled her birthday suit body next to his. "Skip, I hear what you're saying, and I hate that we have to do it like this, but it is what it is. I'm a married woman with a child. I'm the first lady on top of that, so I just can't up and leave him."

"But you said that you don't think you love him anymore, so why can't you leave him? The man doesn't deserve you. He's cool and all with me, but I know him. I know what kind of man he is when he puts down that Bible and steps from behind that pulpit. He was always out for himself. And he's still like that."

Detria propped up a little, turned to the side and looked at Skip. "What do you mean?"

"You knew Stiles back in the day. What do you think I mean?"

"I didn't know him like that. I knew him from going to Holy Rock and he's a couple of years older than me, so I didn't hang around the same circles of friends he did back in high school. Back then, he was a jock, the guy all the girls wanted but couldn't have. He went from one girl to the next. But I thought all of that changed when he went off to school and seminary."

"If you thought that then you were just as naïve as those other females. Stiles did it up in college. He only settled down when he came back home and started preaching at his daddy's church. Then he hooked up with Rena and ended up getting married. But he was still a pistol. You see he up and divorced her don't you. Forget about what the Bible says, 'cause he wasn't thinking about the Bible when he found out old Francesca, Frankie, whatever she called herself was smashing his wife." Skip chuckled. "Man that was wild."

"I didn't know you knew about that."

"You'd have to be on another planet if you didn't hear about that," Skip said and started laughing.

Detria lightly hit him on his chest. "Don't laugh, Skip. It's not funny."

"May not be funny to you, but it's some funny stuff to me. The chick you love, and marry," he added, "has been turned out by your own sister, and you're supposed to be a lady's man? Yeah, that's funny, but hey, you reap what you sow. He broke a lot of females' hearts along the way. And you know what they say, payback is, well, I can't say it how I want to say, so I'll just say payback is something else."

"It's not my intention to hurt Stiles," Detria explained. "All he had to do was love me back. I would have been in his corner one hundred percent. But he, he," she stammered, "keeps part of himself on lock down or something. I can't get through to him. And things got worse after I had his baby. I thought that would have brought us closer together but seems like it's drawing us farther apart. All he wants me to do is stay home and keep a baby. I don't want a life like that, especially if I don't have the love and support of my husband. And sex, well again you know what I told you about that. He wants to do it when he wants to get some relief. He doesn't think about fulfilling my needs. And then he's violent. Sometimes I get scared of him, Skip. I mean really scared." Detria laid her head back against

Skip's bare chest. "I never would have married him if I knew he had a dark side."

"He was known to get a little rowdy with the females back in the day. But I know one thing if he ever hurts you, you better let me know and I'm going to do something bad to Mr. Preacher Man. Something real bad. I don't take to a man beating up on his woman. That's a coward."

"He's raised his hand to me, but thank God he's never hit me. And if he ever does," she said with force, "it'll be his last time. I'll have him locked up behind bars so quick, and he'll never see his daughter again. Holy Rock will be a thing of the past for him because I'll put him on blast so fast he won't know what hit him."

Skip turned slightly and kissed Detria between her eyes. "Like I said, it's a coward who beats a woman. Me, you better believe that I'm no coward. I'm a lover, not a fighter," he whispered as he planted another kiss between her eyes.

"How do I know?" she asked seductively.

"I can show you better than I can tell you," he said as his hands begin to explore every inch of her body.

◊

Detria answered the phone on her desk. It was Stiles.

"Hey, how long have you been here?" he asked.

"Not long. Why? What's up?"

"I was about to go grab a bite to eat, and I saw your car. You want to join me?"

"Ummm, no, I don't think so. You go ahead."

Silence filtered through the phone lines.

"Hello," Detria said, breaking the moment.

"I'm here. What are you doing that you can't break away?" he asked with agitation ringing in his voice and dripping onto Detria's ears. She rolled her eyes up in her head. She was spent from being with Skip all morning. They'd had breakfast in bed too, not to mention the other things they did.

"I have some reports to go over. I need to go through this long list of ministry leaders and see who's going to be doing what and where this Sunday and Wednesday night. And, I have to see if I'm going to have enough volunteers for the lock in this Friday night for the teenagers. It's just a lot I have on my plate. And if you don't want me here all day, then I need to work through lunch. You'll be complaining about the baby being with Mother Brown too long."

"Do what you have to do. I'll talk to you when I get back," Stiles said abruptly.

"I always do," she retorted, as her mind filled with bitter thoughts.

"What's that supposed to mean?"

"Nothing, Stiles. Nothing at all. Anyway, enjoy your lunch." She ended the call before he could say anything else. *You were right, Skip, payback is something else.* And with that thought, Detria remembered a quote she'd memorized from one of her college lit classes. She didn't remember who it was by and she didn't know why she remembered it out of all the quotes and literature passages she had to remember when she was in college, but it was right on the money because it suited how she felt about Stiles. "All the old knives that have rusted in my back, I drive in yours."

24

"I have always considered marriage as the most interesting event of one's life, the foundation of happiness or misery." George Washington

Stiles approached the pulpit after the choir finished their second song. "Turn your Bibles to Ephesians chapter five, and verse thirty-three," he directed the congregation. "Reading from the New King James version, it reads,' Nevertheless, let each one of you in particular so love his own wife as himself, and let the wife *see* that she respects *her* husband."

Detria hoped no one saw her cringe. What was Stiles doing? She'd listened to him practicing his sermon in his study the night before, and the night before that, and she hadn't heard him say one thing about loving your wife and the wife respecting her husband. Did he know something, or suspect something? Surely he didn't. But before she completely dismissed the thought, she quickly turned her head and her eyes locked in on Skip who was seated behind the sound booth live streaming the church service.

"There are three things you should devote yourself to in your marriage. And this works for those of you who aren't married but you're in a relationship. First, be friends. Enjoy one another. Hang out with each other. Spend time together. Establish and nurture your friendship. The Bible says in Ecclesiastes chapter four verses nine through twelve." Stiles looked down at his Bible. "Two are better than one, because they have a good reward for their toil. For if they fall, one will lift up his fellow. But woe to him who is alone when he falls and has not another to lift him up. Again, if two lie together, they keep warm, but how can one keep warm alone? And though a man might prevail against one who is alone, two will withstand him—a threefold cord is not quickly broken. Have a bond of friendship.

"Next, be committed to each other. Don't be ready to throw in the towel every time you have an argument or disagreement. Marriage is a commitment. We run to the divorce courts quick, fast and in a hurry every time we don't agree with something, every time we get mad about stuff that doesn't really matter over the course of a relationship. That's why you need to pray seriously, seek God before you choose your mate. Make sure he's the man God has sent you. Men, make sure she's the woman God has designed for you to be with.

Matthew chapter five verses thirty-one and thirty-two says, 'Whoever divorces his wife, let him give her a certificate of divorce.' But I say to you that everyone who divorces his wife, except on the ground of sexual immorality, makes her commit adultery, and whoever marries a divorced woman commits adultery."

Detria was clearly agitated, but managed to keep her emotions in check. No way would she ever let the members of Holy Rock see her sweat. She had to keep it all together. She looked directly into Stiles' eyes hoping to see some sign that would alert her to what he could have been thinking. There was none. He was preaching just as hard and with fervor like he always did. There were times during the twenty minute sermon when their eyes connected, but it was only for mere seconds. Clearly, this was one of those sermons that Stiles would walk away saying, "That message today was from God to me."

There were times when after having spent long hours studying and researching for a sermon, he would get up on Sunday morning and tell her that the Holy Spirit lead him to preach about something totally different.

The more Stiles preached, the more Detria felt convicted for her adulterous acts. And to think, her mother-in-law had done the same thing. What was it about the Graham men that caused their women to stray? Stiles may not have been a Graham by blood, but still the apple still hadn't fallen too far from the tree.

Detria continued to listen. She was guilty, guilty as sin, but she already knew that once the sermon was over, nothing in her life was going to change. She was going to keep seeing Skip until, well she didn't know how long she was going to see him. But there was no way she would stop until Stiles showed her a different side of him. He had to want to change, realize that he needed to change.

He was too controlling of her and he wanted her to be one of those barefoot and pregnant women. Detria didn't want that. Baby Audrey was enough, and if he thought she was going to lay up and have baby after baby while he ran around parading behind his role of pastor, then he had another thing coming. Plus, she liked Skip. She liked what they had together, even though it was sordid and adulterous on her part. She wasn't perfect. Nobody was perfect. She had her faults and her shortcomings, but she was a good woman but Stiles didn't seem to see that, or he didn't want to see it. She didn't know which one it was, and with each day that passed, she became to care less about his thoughts.

She wouldn't be stupid and wind up getting busted like Audrey did, God rest her soul. Detria felt like she was far too clever for that. She covered her tracks well. Plus, Skip was the kind of man who knew how to keep his mouth shut. He didn't like drama. She laughed out loud before she realized it when she thought about what he said the last time they were in bed together a few days before, "I'm a lover, not a fighter." She hurriedly stifled her laugh by placing her hand over her mouth. The lady next to her looked at her and smiled. Detria patted the woman's hand and smiled back. *If only she knew.*

After church services ended, Stiles and Detria went to lunch at Olive Garden. It was one of the times that they enjoyed each other's company. There was no arguing, fussing or fighting. Detria didn't know if it was because they didn't have Baby Audrey with them or if it was just one of those times they actually had a good time for the sake of having a good time. Mother Brown had asked to keep Baby Audrey so she could take her to her three year old grandbaby's birthday party. It was a welcomed relief for Detria.

"So, you changed your sermon, huh?" she inquired between taking stabs at her garden salad.

"The Holy Spirit led me in a different direction this morning. I wasn't at ease about preaching the sermon I'd prepared. I have to be obedient to God. When I accepted my calling to the ministry, I promised God that I would be his humble servant. Part of that includes listening to Him and obeying Him."

"I didn't say anything was wrong with it, it just took me a little bit by surprise. I didn't know if you were slick trying to talk about our marriage or not." Detria swallowed a forkful of salad and followed it up by taking a swallow of her Skinny Pomegranate Limetta. She loved the mixture of lime, lemon and pomegranate mixed with sparkling water and fresh sliced fruit.

"Don't be so paranoid, Detria," Stiles said and put a hefty portion of his eggplant parmigiana into his mouth. "Unless you have a reason to be," he said with a raised eyebrow.

"Why would I have a reason to be paranoid? All I was thinking about was how we've had our share of rifts lately. I have to admit, it's been hard. Still is, Stiles. Our marriage is far from perfect."

"That's because we've had a lot going on in our lives. These past three years have been tough. Audrey died, Pastor's health concerns, your miscarriage, your pregnancy, Francesca being diagnosed with AIDS. You name it and it seems like it's affected us in some way. And I'm sorry to say that it's mostly had a negative effect on me and I let it spill out into our marriage." Stiles took another forkful of food. "Now this latest round of adversity has really hit home."

"I still can't believe it. Have you talked to Pastor lately? Seems like it's been over a month since I've seen him at Holy Rock. I should have called him, or taken the baby to see him, but I've been so busy. And he hasn't called to check on her, which is really surprising.

"Well, he's fine if you're worried about him."

"I was getting worried, because there was a time nothing could keep him away from his beloved Holy Rock."

Stiles nodded. "Yea, I know, but that's his decision. Skip told me just the other day that he saw Pastor at Kroger. He was with what's her name?"

"Probably Josie," Detria answered. Skip hadn't told her that he'd run into Pastor. She dismissed her trivial thought and continued to listen to her husband.

"Yes, that's who it was. But getting back to what Skip said. He said Pastor told him he had been going to church with his friend, and then Skip said he pointed to Josie and introduced her to him. Guess those two are pretty close," Stiles said.

"Wonder if she knows what went down between you and him, and Francesca."

"I doubt it. If he kept his secrets from his own children, I know he's not about to blurt it to anyone else. At least I wouldn't think so. But then again, who knows what that man will do. I never thought he'd be the kind of person who would purposely deceive his own family either, but he did."

"Well, you know what you have to do," Detria remarked.

Stiles stopped messing around with his food and eyed Detria curiously. "What?" he asked her.

"Forgive him. Plain and simple."

"Tell me something I don't already know. I've prayed about it, ever since it happened. I called him a few days after that, but I, well, I guess I haven't truly forgiven him in my heart because I didn't have one kind word to say to him. On the contrary, I went off on him again."

"Well, the thing is, you're not going to be able to move forward if you don't let it go. And it's obvious that he forgave Audrey. He stayed with her knowing the child she had wasn't his. And every time I was around them as a couple, they doted on one another like they were the happiest married couple in the world."

"You're right about that. And, who knows, maybe they were. I mean it didn't seem like he hated her, and she definitely acted like he was the icing on her favorite cake."

"Exactly, so pray about it some more and do whatever God directs you to do," Detria advised.

"Thanks," he told her.

"For what?" she asked him.

"You've always been a great listener, and you give good advice." He immediately went into his spiel. "Look, I know I'm not the easiest guy to love. I know I have some anger issues and probably some control issues too, but I really do want our marriage to work, Detria."

Detria's defenses subsided somewhat as she listened. This was the Stiles she'd fallen for. The one who was sensitive and caring. But during their marriage she had begun to see far less of this side of him. It was almost like he had a good twin and an evil twin, and most of the time the evil twin reigned.

"Are you listening to me?" he asked.

"Yes, I'm listening to you. And I want our marriage to work too. I'll be the first to admit that I'm not perfect either. I know you expected me to be more, well more of a stay-at-home type of wife and mother. One who loves to be at home with the kids type of wife, and I wish I could be that person. But I'm not. Don't get me wrong. I love our daughter. And maybe one day we can give her a brother or sister like you want, but even if we do have other children, I still don't see myself being the house-wifey type. That's not me. That's not who I am, Stiles. And if you can't deal with that, then I don't know what the future holds for us."

"I'm going to be honest. I do have some serious concerns when it comes to your, quote unquote," Stiles said while gesturing with his hands, "unconventional way of motherhood. I thought you would love being at home raising our daughter. And you never told me that you didn't want to play that role. So I'm sorry for assuming that you would be that kind of wife, that kind of mother."

Detria did a show of hands. "Hold, up. I'm not putting all the blame on you. After all, a closed mouth doesn't get fed, so I should have told you in the beginning, even while I was carrying Baby Audrey, that I did not want to sign up for being a full-time housewife and mother. But I didn't, and so here we are. Almost at a crossroads of sort. "

"But it's not too late for us to make this work. Or is it?" he looked at Detria.

That would mean breaking things off with Skip. Do I want to do that? Do I really want to have more kids with Stiles? Keep being the First Lady?

Stiles looked disappointed when Detria hesitated.

"No, I...I don't think it's too late. I don't think it's too late at all," she said slowly, almost with a tinge of uncertainty ringing in her words.

Stiles reached across the table and caressed her cheek while Detria thought about how she might really have to break things off with Skip if she planned on giving her marriage a real chance to work.

25

“They say that blood is thicker than water. Maybe that's why we battle our own with more energy and gusto than we would ever expend on strangers.” David Assael

Francesca curled up in the center of her bed and wept. The opened letter from the adoption agency was laced with fancy words ladened with nothing but heartbreak for Francesca. They had denied her and Tim. She would never be able to be a mom. She wanted to have that chance so badly, a chance to show a child what being a real mother was supposed to be like. But thanks to her sickness, though the letter didn’t come out and say it, she wouldn’t know what it felt like to hold a child in her arms, or to love a child unconditionally.

Tim had tried to explain to her that they could be surrogate parents to his sisters' kids, or to the vast array of cousins he had in his family. But that wouldn't be the same for Francesca. She wanted to hear a child call her mother and Tim father.

"Father, I know I've messed up my life. I know I'm the blame for being laid up here with AIDS. I know all of the mistakes and screw-up's I've made. But God, I've tried to turn my life around. I've tried to be a better person." Francesca wiped tears from her eyes as she looked upward. "You said you would forgive me if I confessed my sins, and I did. So why, why couldn't you let me have just one, one child to love? Why do I have to pay for my past over and over again?"

She read the letter several times before balling it up in her fists and throwing it to the other side of the bedroom. She continued to cry until she had no more tears left. Her conversation with God continued as she questioned the reason for her existence and purpose in life.

◊

"What's up, Pretty Lady?" Skip asked.

"Skip, how many times do I have to tell you. We can't see each other anymore. I'm trying to give my marriage a fair shake."

Detria had called Skip up the day after she and Stiles discussed the state of their marriage. That had been two weeks ago, and Skip was still not cutting her any slack. He was persistent and Detria was slowly succumbing to his pleas though she hadn't given in to him.

"And I told you, you don't want to be with Stiles. So why are you making yourself miserable trying? Come on, Detria. One last time. Meet me one last time, baby.

And I promise, if you'll just do this one thing for me, I won't bother you again. I'll speak to you when I see you, do what I can to help you around the church, whatever I have to do, but I won't bother you about me and you again. Just say you'll meet me."

Detria listened to him pleading with her on the other end of the telephone line. He sounded so sincere. And she didn't want to admit it to him, but she missed him. She missed him a lot. Skip had been emailing her, texting her and pulling her to the side at Holy Rock every chance he got. She couldn't hold back any longer.

"Okay, but I'm telling you, this is going to be it. We can't do this anymore."

"Okay, baby. Meet me at our spot at say, two, two-thirty?"

"Two-thirty will be better. I have to go over some paperwork for the Children's Ministry and check my emails and stuff too. And I have to see if Mother Brown can watch Audrey."

"Straight. Just text me when you're on your way."

"I will," she said and ended their call.

She went into Stiles' office to check her emails because she had left hers in the car, and didn't feel like going to get it. "Just have to use yours. You'll never know the difference," she said out loud. Stiles was ticky about his computer because he kept all of his sermons and messages on it. It was off limits to her, and she didn't mind since she had her own.

She sat at his desk, and that's when she noticed he had left it on, something he rarely if ever did. "He must have really been in a hurry this morning to leave this on."

Detria clicked the space bar and the computer screen came on. His email box was open, definitely much to her surprise. She didn't know his password and he didn't know hers, but no password was needed because his mailbox was wide open. She didn't know why it hadn't timed out.

She began scrolling through the dozens of emails, scanning the subject lines. *If you go looking for trouble, trouble will find you*, she seemed to hear a voice say in her mind. She ignored it. And find it she did. Her complexion turned two shades darker when she saw and read the emails from Stiles' ex.

Stop emailing me! I don't want anything to do with you, Stiles. At the end of the email she read what Stiles had sent to Rena. *Rena, I was thinking about you today. I hope you're doing well. You deserve to be happy.*

Another one read, *I'm trying to live my life without you interfering in it....* And Stiles message to her said, *Rena, I keep thinking about how I messed up a good thing with you. I know I've said it a hundred times before, but I have to say it again, I'm sorry. I can't help but think how things might have turned out had I not been so stupid back then. I know we're both married now, and I don't mean to act like a stalker or anything, but just know that you'll always hold a special place in my heart. You'll always have a piece of me.*

Still a third one said, *How do you think your wife would feel if she knew you were doing this?*

Stiles: *I tried to call you but you've changed your cell number. I called your parents, but they wouldn't tell me how I could get in touch with you. I don't mean to be a nuisance; I just wanted to see how you were doing. I hope you're happy. I hope he's treating you right...*

Detria couldn't cry. Her fingers were shaking as she scrolled through the emails. She felt like a fool. She knew he still loved Rena and this was the proof. She went into his Sent box and saw dozens and dozens of email messages he'd been sending to Rena.

"I'm pregnant with my HUSBAND'S child. I am not your wife anymore. What part of I don't love you or want you don't you understand? Do not, and I mean do not try to contact me anymore. I don't want to tell your wife, but if you keep trying to contact me, you leave me no choice. MRS. RENA BECTON!!!!!"

The last email she read was one Stiles had sent Rena just a few days prior. *"Rena, I don't know what was wrong with me. I had no right to hound you the way I did. You deserve to be happy. And I hope that you are. I'm glad to hear about your pregnancy. I know you're going to enjoy being a mother, and you're going to make a great one too. I won't bother you again. I hope you can find it in your heart to forgive me for everything. Enjoy your life. May God bless you and keep you. Stiles*

"What are you doing?" Stiles yelled, starling Detria. Her head popped around at the sound of his voice.

"What are you doing on my computer?" he barked.

"What are you doing home?" she yelled back.

"Don't dodge my question," he said and walked over to where she sat.

Detria noticed how huge his pupils had grown when he saw his email open.

"Don't look so surprised," she bit. "You left your computer on, you dogg, you." She jumped up from her seated position and spewed endless profanities at her husband. "All this mess about you want to make our marriage work. You're nothing but a liar."

Stiles stood rigid. “I do want our marriage to work. Whatever you think is going on, isn’t.”

Detria released a wicked kind of laugh. “You really take me for a fool, don’t you? Well, I’m nobody’s fool, Stiles. I never have been and I’m not about to start now. You can have your precious little Rena, but from the responses to your emails, it’s not likely that she’s ready to come running back to you,” Detria screamed and spat.

She took two steps to the side and started to walk off but Stiles grabbed hold of her elbow.

“Wait, Detria. Please, let me explain. I sent those emails when we were going through our turmoil. I felt like our marriage was over. I was lonely and miserable, but that’s not how I feel now, Detria. I love you. You have to believe me. Please,” he begged while keeping a tight grip on her elbow.

“Turn me a loose. You’re hurting me,” she yelled. “You don’t want this marriage. You want someone who you’ll never have again, Stiles. What part of what the woman is telling you don’t you believe? She has a husband. She is pregnant with his child. Not yours. She’s changed her number, Stiles just so she won’t be bothered by the likes of you. You’re so sickening. Who are you?”

“I’m human. I messed up,” he said and tears began streaming down his face. “Please, Detria. Please forgive me.”

Detria managed to jerk away from his grasp. She stormed out of the study and fled to their bedroom, turning the lock behind her. She got her overnight bag out of the walk-in closet and quickly packed a few items in it while Stiles begged for forgiveness from the other side.

When she opened the door, she dashed past him and hurried down the steps.

"Where are you going?" he asked.

"Away from you. I can't stay here. Not now. I need some time to think. I'll call Mother Brown and see if she'll watch the baby for a while. I'm in no shape to take care of her tonight, not after this." She rolled her reddening eyes at Stiles. She walked into the downstairs guest room and went inside and removed Audrey out of her porta-crib. The little girl seemed content as she played with her toys and sucked on her pacifier.

"Don't do this, Detria. Please. We can work this out without you leaving our home, and taking our daughter."

She didn't say a word, but instead she gathered some items out of the room and put them inside Baby Audrey's diaper bag that was on the nightstand.

"I'm not doing anything; it's you who caused this." She held the baby on her hip along with the other two bags she had and went into the kitchen and got several bottles out of the side by side refrigerator. "You're so wrapped up in yourself that you can't see the pain you're causing me. It always has to be all about you. Well, no more, Stiles Graham. You don't listen when I talk, maybe you'll listen when I walk," she said and walked off.

Next, with Stiles at her footsteps she headed for the garage. He didn't try to stop her physically, but instead tried to keep her from leaving him with his pleas. Detria ignored him, got the baby in the car and then followed suit. She punched the remote control and the garage door came up. Turning the ignition on, she proceeded to back out of the garage.

"Detria, you know the Bible. The Bible says, "Don't let the sun go down upon your wrath. Let's talk about this, sweetheart. Please, Detria. Do not be quickly provoked in your spirit, for anger resides in the lap of fools." he continued to spout scriptures as Detria put the car in gear and drove off and up the street.

◊

"Didn't I tell you that it wasn't going to work out between you two?" Skip said. "I don't know why you still put up with him."

Detria rested her head against Skip's chest. "I do not want to be a statistic, that's why. When I got married, it was supposed to be until death do us part. My parents have been married almost fifty years and I'm sure they've been through some tough times. But they're still together."

"But I bet your daddy didn't treat your mother the way Stiles is treating you either. The man is flat out disrespecting you, Detria." Skip expressed.

"It's not like I'm an angel, you know. Look at me," she said. "I'm here crying on another man's shoulder; my husband's friend at that."

"He doesn't know that. And you have every right to be with me after what he's putting you through." Skip pushed her away gently and then looked into Detria's eyes that had for the first time since arguing with Stiles, started to overflow with tears. "It's all right baby. I'm here. I'm going to make everything all right. Okay?" he said while kissing her face.

Detria gave in. She wondered why she didn't feel guilt for the relief she felt. Maybe Skip was right Maybe her marriage was beyond repair. She shivered as Skip gently eased her down on the hotel bed. His touch was light as he expertly explored her body, transporting her to a place of pleasure.

◊

Pastor dialed Francesca's number again and again, much like he'd done the past few months, and again the phone went straight to an automated voicemail. He had tried unsuccessfully to bring his family back together but he failed. He was too humiliated to go to Holy Rock, the very church he'd founded. It didn't feel right any longer. It was like he had no place there. The ties that bind seemed to be forever broken, and Pastor didn't know if they would ever be able to be repaired.

He put the cordless phone back on its charging base before he sat down in his chair and picked up his Bible. His spirit felt like it had been crushed and that there was no way for him to regain footage. In a matter of moments, he'd managed to tear his family structure apart with his words.

"Audrey," he cried. "Why? What have I done? What have I done?" He sobbed while still clutching the Bible.

He picked up the phone again. This time he dialed Stiles' phone. He answered on the second ring.

"Stiles, son. Please, don't' hang up. We need to talk."

"I agree. I need to talk to you, too. I'm on my way over there."

"Certainly," Pastor said. "Thank you, Lord," said Pastor. Stiles had finally answered his call. Pastor's spirit leaped with joy. He flipped through his Bible and stopped when he came to another one of his favorite scriptures. "Let not your heart be troubled," he began to read.

Stiles rushed to Pastor's apartment. He had nowhere else to turn, no one who he wanted to confide in. It was time for him to, at least momentarily, put the past behind him. He needed Pastor's words of wisdom. No matter how bad he felt Pastor had messed up, he needed the man he'd always known as father.

Pastor listened to Stiles tell him everything that had happened between him and Detria.

He is so much like his mother, Pastor thought. Audrey could make some of the biggest mistakes and then turn around and beg for forgiveness like it was the end of the world. And each and every time, Pastor would forgive her. Pastor believed that Detria would end up being just like him. Stiles, again like Audrey, had a way with words, and a way of pulling at one's heart strings. Unless Detria was tougher than Pastor thought, she would be back in the arms of her husband before she would realize it herself.

"Give her some time, son. She's been hurt," Pastor told him. "Rena has been dogging her footsteps ever since the two of you met. She probably feels like she's always living in her shadows. And I sympathize with her. The girl can't be sure if you really love her or not. And seeing all those emails between the two of you, well, that's a hard pill to swallow. You have got to let Rena go, son. She's not your wife anymore. Detria is. You need to concentrate on building your marriage, and making a stable family environment for Baby Audrey and any future children you might have. It's going to take some time. You're going to have to spend every moment trying to rebuild trust in your marriage."

"But how?" asked Stiles. "How can I ever make her understand that I love her, and that I'm sorry. I don't know why I keep running to my past. I mean, I know

Rena has moved on, and so have I. But I keep on going back, or at least trying to go back. Like I'm trying to hold on to a piece of my yesterday. But why? I don't understand it," Stiles explained.

"You're living in the 'what-if' mode. And what if will get you in a lot of serious trouble. I had to release a lot during my marriage. I could have held on to the past, divorced your mother because I had every right to do so. But I chose not to. I had to look at the bigger picture."

"And what was that?" Stiles asked.

"I had to look at me," Pastor said and pointed to himself. "Maybe I didn't go out and have an affair on Audrey, but I might as well had. I was married to Holy Rock, the church I built from not only the ground up but I built that membership. It was my world, my life. I put it before my marriage, my family, and I believe I put it before God. And God wasn't pleased. He wasn't pleased at all. I guess that's why I had to forgive her. She forgave me over and over again for being an absentee husband, lover, friend, father and so much more. How could I not forgive her. And I've done it again."

"How?" Stiles asked.

"Because this time I put myself ahead of you and Francesca. I was too busy wanting to keep my dignity that I was willing to spill your mother's secrets, secrets I promised to take to my grave."

Stiles listened intently to Pastor. The more he listened, the more Stiles understood how badly he had hurt his wife, just like Audrey had hurt Pastor all those years ago. Stiles soon began to realize that he really didn't want to get back with Rena. Instead, he was caught up in the fantasy of having someone, something he couldn't have. And now, he may have lost Detria in the process.

"You're going to have to seek God's face. Ask God to lead you and guide you. And you know he will."

Stiles remained silent.

"If you love your wife, fight for her. Show her that it's her and nobody else that you want to be with."

Stiles remained at Pastor's apartment until late in the afternoon. While he was there, he had tried calling Detria several times, but she didn't answer. He reached Mother Brown. Detria had left their daughter with her.

"It's time I leave," Stiles told Pastor. "I'm going to pick up my daughter, and then I'm going to go home and make preparations for my wife to come back home."

"Good," Pastor said as he stood up and patted Stiles on his back. "Therefore I say to *you*, all things for which *you* pray and ask, *believe that you have received* them, and they *will* be granted *you*."

Stiles nodded, confirming the scripture Pastor quoted, he said, "Mark eleven twenty-four." He walked toward the door, stopped and turned to face Pastor who had followed behind him. "I'm sorry. Will you forgive me for the way I talked to you, disrespected you. I've been wrong on so many levels. Who am I to judge you? I have no real right or reason to be angry with you over the sins of my mother. What happened was between the two of you and God."

Pastor patted Stiles on the back and then reached out and grabbed him, pulling him into a father-son hug. Tears streamed as he held on to Stiles like his life depended on it.

Asking for forgiveness can be hard to do, but Stiles slowly started to realize that if he expected or hoped for

Detria to forgive him, he had to have a forgiving spirit, and it started with forgiving his entire family.

26

"Be positive! It's not about who hurt you and broke you down. It's about who was always there and made you smile again!" Unknown

Tim stared at Francesca sitting across from him at their kitchen table. Ever since they'd been turned down for adoption, Francesca had been in a funk. He'd tried all kinds of things to help her cheer up but she seemed to be up one day and totally down the next. Today his parents were coming to visit, and Tim hoped that would help bring her around some.

Francesca loved Tim's parents and they loved her. They were going to bring one of his nieces along with them. Maybe Francesca would enjoy that. At least he hoped that she would.

"Honey, you've barely touched your lunch. You need to eat. You want to stay healthy don't you?"

Francesca slightly nodded, then toyed around with the veggie burger Tim had prepared for her. "I know, but I just don't have an appetite right now."

"Baby, you're going to have to pull yourself up out of this depression. It's not good for you. I know you're hurt about the adoption agency's decision, but God is in control. He knows what's best for us. Something will break for us, Francesca. You have to believe that, baby. Please, don't do this to yourself."

She looked into Tim's eyes and traces of a smile filtered across her face. "You're right, but it's just so hard. I was so pumped up, thinking we were going to have the chance to be parents. And I know how much having a child would mean to you."

"This isn't about me. It's about us. I don't want anything apart from you, baby. I'm concerned about you. Would it have been great to have a little one running around the house? Sure it would. But everything is working out the way it's supposed to. We can't see what's ahead but God can, and that's who we should rely on."

"I know, Tim. And I promise that I'm going to make an effort to move forward from this." Francesca pushed back from the table and stood up. "What time do you think your parents will be here?"

"Around three o'clock. They're bringing Kyra with them."

Francesca's face lit up. Kyra was five years old and was adorable. She was Tim's oldest sister's little girl and she loved to hang around her grandparents. Francesca couldn't wait to see her and spend time with the little girl.

"They're bringing Kyra? I'm glad to hear that. That little girl is such a hoot. She's so smart it's like she's been here before," Francesca said and giggled.

"See, that's my girl. I love to see you smile," Tim said and got up and walked up to Francesca. He kissed the crown of her head and hugged her around the waist.

Her face quickly turned from a smile to a serious look. "If only I had had the kind of relationship with my parents that you have with yours, maybe my life would have turned out better. Don't you think?" She turned and faced Tim.

"I think you dwell too much on yesterday. I keep telling you to let the past stay in the past. Now if you want to reach out to Stiles and Pastor, that's a whole different story. I know they would love to—"

Francesca covered his lips with her hand. "No, you already know that I'm not going to do that. I forgive them, and I love them, but I don't want them in my inner circle. At least not right now. Maybe one day down the line, I can invite them back into my life, but there's too much pain connected with them, Tim. And I'm tired of hurting."

Tim gently removed her hand from his mouth and kissed it. "I know, and I understand. I won't bring it up anymore. Now, what do you say we get everything ready for mom and dad, and little Miss Kyra. If we're going to grill like you said we were going to do, then we need to go to the farmer's market and get some fresh vegetables."

"Sounds good. I'm ready whenever you are."

"Okay, let's do this."

◊

Detria returned home after being gone for a week. After talking to her parents and her sister, she made the decision to give her marriage one last try. Skip was dead set against it, but she explained to him that she owed that much to her marriage. Finally, he relented, told her he understood but made it clear that if she needed a strong shoulder to cry on, that he would be there for her.

"I thought we'd go away for a few days. Just the two of us," Stiles told Detria when he returned home from the university that evening.

Detria was planted in front of her laptop working on a new ministry she wanted to implement at Holy Rock. It was going to be an extension to the Marriage Ministry.

She stopped typing and looked at him. "Go where? And what about church?"

"Myrtle Beach. And as for church, even the pastor needs some time off every now and then. One thing we have at Holy Rock that I'm glad about is we have some good, faithful and anointed associate ministers. So church will go on. But right now, I want to spend every moment I can making up for all the hurt and pain I've caused you. I want you to trust me again, Detria."

Detria was torn. She said she wanted her marriage to work, but yet she didn't know if Stiles could make her happy anymore. The past year had revealed a lot of things about him that she wasn't exactly pleased about. His violent tendencies were something that frightened her. Would there come a time when he would strike her? And the fact that he wanted a housewife, a full time mother to his children, well Detria didn't know if she could ever be that woman.

Then there was Skip. She didn't want to say that she was in love with him, but she did have strong feelings for him. And Skip was not one to give up easily. She liked the way he treated her. She liked the way he held her and showed concern toward her. She liked everything about Skip Madison. But was Skip just a fantasy that would fade away. Was the grass really that much greener on Skip's side of the fence?

And what did she have with Stiles? They had a child together, a beautiful home, and she was the first lady. She loved the role and the attention she received from being the wife of Stiles Graham. She had a lot to think about.

"Stiles, I don't know if our marriage can be saved. We've grown so far apart. I just don't know if I'm the woman you really want. I can't compete with your ex-wife. I'm not her. I will never be her. And I do not want to be her. I'm me, Detria—"

"Graham," Stiles finished. "You're Detria Graham, my lady, the first lady of Holy Rock Church, the mother of my precious daughter. You're beautiful, and funny. You're a great listener. You are so many wonderful things, Detria."

"I don't know what to say. I'm shocked by all of this."

"I know you are, but I mean every word of it." Stiles sat down next to her. "I know it's going to take time for you to believe in me again, for you to believe that we can make this work, but I'm willing, Detria. God knows I'm willing to do whatever it takes," he said with genuine sincerity.

"Let's do it then. I've been wanting to go to Myrtle Beach for the longest time."

"I know," Stiles said. "Which is exactly why I chose it. I've looked into some great hotels, and I already talked to Mother Brown about taking care of Baby Audrey. We'll only be gone a week so she said it was no problem."

"Seems like you've already thought of everything," Detria said and forced a smiled. "How did you know I would say yes?"

"I didn't, but God knows I've been praying about it for a minute." He laughed. "We're going to have a great time making up."

Detria joined him in laughter. "Ohhh, is that right?"

"Yes," he answered before scooping her in his arms and kissing her passionately. "What do you say we start practicing on what we're going to do when we get to Myrtle Beach," he teased seductively.

He nibbled on her earlobes, then picked up her laptop and placed it on the other side of him. His hands played jazz with her body, and Detria didn't deny him access. Maybe, just maybe they had a chance after all.

Seven Months Later

Family quarrels are bitter things. They don't go according to any rules. They're not like aches or wounds; they're more like splits in the skin that won't heal because there's not enough material. F. S. Fitzgerald.

Rena and Robert bundled up the twins and put them in their car seats, while Isabelle and Robbie got in the van on their own. Isabelle got in her booster seat while Robbie climbed in his.

"Fasten your belts, Robbie and Isabelle," Robert reminded them.

"Are we going to church?" Isabelle asked.

"No, Isabelle, we aren't going to church."

"Then why are all dressed up?" she asked.

"Honey," Robert explained. "Didn't we tell you and Robbie that today is a very special day? Today, you're going to officially have Rena as your mother."

"Oh, yeah, I know that. But I thought she was already our mother," Isabelle continued to question.

"She is, but we have to have a judge tell us too. Remember what we told you the first time we talked to the judge?"

"Um hum," Isabelle replied. "I remember now."

Rena and Robert looked at each other, shook their heads and smiled.

"Let me help you with the twins," Rena told Robert who was trying to secure the latch on their car seats. "These things can be hard to fasten sometimes."

"Yeah, tell me about it," Robert said.

"There you go Rachel and Riana, all fastened," she said to the precious identical twin girls.

The family of four arrived at the courthouse for the official adoption papers to be signed.

Rena was on cloud nine. She had given birth to two healthy, beautiful babies, she had a husband who loved her, and now within a matter of hours, she would be declared the legal mother of Isabelle and Robbie. It felt good to have her life back on track and moving in such a positive manner. She hadn't heard anything more from Stiles since his last email months ago telling her he wouldn't be bothering her again. And he hadn't.

She enjoyed each day she spent taking care of the twins along with Isabelle and Robbie.

They left the courthouse and headed to Robert's sister's house to celebrate the official adoption among family and friends.

"I love you, Robert Becton," she said as they drove along the highway.

"I love you more, Mrs. Becton, the fabulous, beautiful mother of my children," he answered before he leaned over and kissed her.

◊

Detria stood in front of the floor to ceiling mirror and surveyed herself. She had questions for the reflection staring back at her. "How long can I keep doing this? She asked herself. "Can this marriage really be saved?"

She smiled at the reflection. "Yes, yes it can," she answered herself. "You can do this, girl," she told the woman in the mirror. "You can do it. You just have to try, keep praying and do not fall weak to Skip Madison," she fussed at her reflection.

The past several months had proven to be tough for her and Stiles. At first, she was ready to call it quits, but something within told her to hold on. She had even talked to Brooke and told her about the problems she and Stiles had been having. She purposely left off the part about her affair with Skip.

Brooke advised her not to give up on her marriage because marriage was sacred and required a life time of commitment to one another.

It wasn't exactly the advice Detria wanted to hear, but she nevertheless, took her sister to heart. Brooke knew what she was talking about in Detria's eyes, because she and her husband had two boys and had been married for twelve years.

As for her weakness: Skip Madison - Detria had given in to him twice since her recommitment to her marriage. She still missed him but she was trying to be strong. There was no way she could just dismiss him totally out of her life because of their connection to Holy Rock. So they talked mostly at church, and occasionally on the phone or via text. But sleeping with him, she finally promised God and herself that she wouldn't go down that road again. She didn't want to end up like her mother-in-law with dark, deep secrets left behind to be exposed to her family.

"You can do this," she said to the woman in the mirror. "You can make this work. You are making this work."

She turned and went to check on Baby Audrey who was growing up fast, and had started walking a week prior. The little girl was getting into everything. Detria had finally begun to enjoy motherhood. Brooke had told her that as Baby Audrey began to get older, things would get better, and they had.

Detria chose to remain the church administrator at Holy Rock rather than return to her former job as a nutritionist. Her hours at the church were self-made, and afforded Detria the freedom she enjoyed and the career she craved.

The more time she spent at the church, the more time she wanted to spend at the church. Her marriage was getting better, and like a daily mantra she constantly told herself that being married to Stiles wasn't so bad.

◊

Stiles made the decision to resign from his position at the University so he could devote more time with his family. He desperately wanted his marriage to work and to last. He'd also started talking to a trusted preacher friend several months prior about his anger issues.

Much to his pleasant surprise, he had begun to display his anger in a healthier way rather than through violent outbursts. It made for a stronger relationship between him and Detria.

He had long since stopped making contact with Rena. He had finally come to terms with the fact that his past needed to be left behind, and Rena was part of his past. She had moved on with her life and so had he. It was time to devote himself fully to his relationship with Detria, his daughter, and Holy Rock.

Stiles desired to have more children one day, and he hoped that not too far down the road that Detria would agree. He still wasn't wholeheartedly satisfied with her mothering skills, but he believed that she loved Baby Audrey. He saw her trying to be a better mother to their daughter, and that in and of itself encouraged him to give his marriage a chance. Now that he was around more, he was able to spend more time with Baby Audrey, and that made it less stressful on his wife.

He sought God's forgiveness and asked that God make him a better man. He had his faults, plenty of them, he admitted to his preacher friend and to God. He realized that he had issues with forgiveness. He always preached about it, but he seemed to fall short from following his own teaching. And then there were the problems with Audrey and Francesca. Why did he all but close his eyes to his sister's ill treatment by their mother? He continued to toy with the answers to his own questions. There were still too many loopholes for him to be able to decipher what was what.

He couldn't quite figure out in his mind why Audrey kept those newspaper articles and lied about being raped, when she knew that Francesca was her lover's baby...and not some rapist. Unless, unless she had actually been raped like she said. Stiles couldn't figure it out.

There was no doubt in his mind that she'd had an affair like Pastor said, but still Stiles wrestled with what was fact and what was fiction when it came to his dear mother, God rest her soul. Now it was too late to ever know the real truth. There was no way to ever be certain what Audrey was thinking back then, but he came to the conclusion that it was time to let it all die along with her, even though what she said in the letter and what Pastor divulged was hard to digest.

Stiles loved Audrey, and why wouldn't he? She was his mother after all, but he understood and now truly believed that Audrey Graham had some serious issues that she struggled with when she was here on this earth. She was gone now, but her secrets, her past deeds had still managed to destroy their family even from the grave. It was going to take time, a long time before their family could completely heal or even mend.

The wedge it placed in his relationship with Francesca was huge and Stiles didn't know if Francesca would ever come to terms with it. He could only pray that one day she would forgive him, their mother and Pastor.

Stiles contemplated his ways too. He wasn't exactly a model guy. He had his faults and his secrets too. If the church family ever knew that he had an anger management problem they would see him in a far different light. Maybe he did have ways like Audrey. Longtime members of Holy Rock often told him he reminded them of First Lady Audrey Graham, and that he had a lot of her ways. He didn't know if he should take that as a compliment or not. Maybe he saw in his mother only what he wanted to see. And when it came to his relationship with his sister, he finally owned up to the truth, that he had not exactly been a star brother while they were growing up. In his own way, he mistreated Francesca too. No wonder she rebelled against all of them. She'd had no one to turn to. No one whom she could trust.

And Pastor, well Stiles thought that he should have let sleeping dogs lie . Why did he have to tell him and Francesca about Audrey's affair? Love can make a person do foolish things, and the hurt Pastor had harbored all the years of their marriage came to a head under the mounting pressure he felt. It was probably good that Pastor finally got his true feelings about his darling wife off his chest. Now he hopefully could move on with his life as well.

Anyway, Stiles soon reasoned that just like the word of God stated, 'All things work together for good...'

"Honey, are you ready?" he asked as he walked up on Detria and rubbed his lips against her neck.

"Yes, I'm ready." She took hold of Baby Audrey's hand and led her toward the kitchen.

"Come on, pretty lady," she said to her daughter. "It's time to go see your granddaddy get married."

Stiles laughed.

"Can you believe it? Pastor is getting married. I'm glad for him. Sister Josie is a good catch," he remarked.

"I think so too. She loves that man."

"Yes, she does, and I believe he loves her. I'm glad he's found someone who he can be happy with again," Stiles commented.

"I wish Francesca and Tim had come down."

"She's changed her phone number, so I couldn't call her. Pastor said that he mailed her an invitation but he never heard back from her."

"I just hope she's doing okay," Detria remarked.
"Me too," Stiles replied.

◊

Francesca had been feeling better with each day that passed. She was still sticking to her diet and lifestyle changes.

She had recently received an invitation from Pastor about his impending marriage but decided that her life was going better without interference from Pastor and Stiles.

"Tim," she called from the kitchen. "Do you want some lemonade? I just made it," she told him.

Tim was in his office working on a design project. He was glad to see his wife doing better, feeling better and sounding better. Their marriage was more than he could have ever expected and that he was truly grateful to God for.

"Yes, I'd love a glass," he replied.

"Okay, I'll bring it to you in just a sec," she answered.

Maybe she had made many mistakes, costly mistakes in her life, but now Francesca was ready to move forward, to enjoy the life, the second chance that she'd been given. She was far from being perfect, and she understood that one day she would have to reach out to her family, if for no other reason but to let them know that she had forgiven them.

After all, she'd been given a new slate on life so who was she not to do the same for others, especially her family.

Words From The Author

"Oh what a tangled web we weave, when first we practice to deceive." This quotation by Sir Walter Scott rings true. Deceit is nothing but a tangled web. It leads to trouble, heartache and heartbreak. Did you know that a spider's web is so strong that it is said to be the equivalent of steel! That's amazing to me. When I see a spider web, at first glance it looks delicate, like it can be easily torn apart. But if you've ever seen an insect fly into a spider's web, you'll notice that it is virtually impossible for it to break loose. It is trapped and unless the spider decides to eat it right away, it is subject to suffering for a long period of time, and eventually dying.

That's how deep and dangerous deception can be. Deceit can kill your spirit, wound the heart, tear apart families like it did in the Graham family. The grip of deceit is stronger than steel!

Who can we say is the one who was actually deceitful in the My Son's series? Is it First Lady Audrey? Maybe it is Stiles. Then again, could it be Pastor or Detria? Who do you place the blame on?

I place the blame on the devil. The devil is like a roaring lion wandering around seeking whom he may devour. How does he do this unless he does it through deceitful practices. He is the father of lies. There is no good thing about him. He parades around in shoes of deception and clothes of betrayal.

Each of the characters in the My Son's Series has been affected in some way by deceit. They have been tricked, lied to, lied on, and lied about. They have been the enemy, the deceiver, the hater and the trickster. But they have also expressed love, forgiveness, faith and trust. They are believers like many of us, but reading about them, you might think differently. Again, like us because sometimes people can't tell by looking at us, listening to us, and being around us that we profess to be children of God.

We all are imperfect creatures, which is why God chose to die for us, even while we were yet sinners. We needed and continue to need an advocate, an intercessor, someone who will plead our case even when we do awful things. That advocate is Jesus Christ. Wow, am I so glad I have him on my side. If I did not I would suffer hell and damnation because of my terrible sin nature.

We all need rescuing from the tangled web that others weave for us and from the web that we sometimes weave for others and then the web we even weave for ourselves. We need to ask to be delivered continually from the web of deceit that entraps us.

Don't be so quick to look and judge others for the mistakes they make in life, or the bad choices they make. Instead, try to remember that you too have flaws and imperfections. You too have done something dreadful and awful, thought something that you shouldn't have, said something that you shouldn't have, acted in a way that you shouldn't have. You too have hurt someone, probably messed over someone, whether it was intentional or not. The fact remains that we all have mess in our lives, and it is only by God's grace and his mercy that is new every morning, that we can call ourselves believers and Christians.

So, you who call yourselves children of the Most High God, learn how to turn the other cheek. Learn how to forgive even when you don't want to forgive. What you see on the outside is not always what the truth is. We never know what is going on in a person's life. What we should do is to love others unconditionally. Treat others the way we truly want to be treated.

Audrey Graham carried secrets to the grave that spilled over out of the grave. Her deceitful ways far outlived her. I don't know about you, but I don't want to die being an Audrey. I don't want the dirt of my past to ruin the future of those who live on.

So, take the time now to reevaluate your life. If there is anything you have not repented for, or asked forgiveness for, I urge you to do so now. If there is someone you have wronged along life's journey, whether you are young or old, black or white, male or female, seek that person's forgiveness because true love really does mean saying you're sorry.

Matthew 7:1-5 "Judge not, that you be not judged. 2 "For with what judgment you judge, you will be judged; and with the measure you use, it will be measured back to you. 3 "And why do you look at the speck in your brother's eye, but do not consider the plank in your own eye? 4 "Or how can you say to your brother, 'Let me remove the speck from your eye'; and look, a plank is in your own eye? 5 "Hypocrite! First remove the plank from your own eye, and then you will see clearly to remove the speck out of your brother's eye

Discussion Questions

1. Should parents keep secrets from their children? Why or why not?
2. Do you think Stiles is too controlling?"
3. Does Stiles expect too much from Detria when it comes to the time she spends with Baby Audrey? Why or Why not?
4. What do you honestly think about Detria? Is she in love with Stiles?
5. What kind of mother is Detria in your opinion?
6. Has Francesca really changed her ways? Why or Why not?
7. Why would Pastor tell Francesca and Stiles about Audrey's real past?
8. How do you view Pastor in this installment of the My Son's series?
9. Discuss the relationship between Detria and Skip.
10. Why do you think Audrey wrote that letter and said the things she said?

11. Do you believe Audrey was telling the truth in the letter she wrote? Or do you believe the story Pastor told Francesca and Stiles about Audrey? Why or Why not?

12. Discuss the relationship between Stiles and Rena.

13. Has Rena finally moved on in her life? Why or Why not?

14. Do you believe Francesca and Tim should have been approved to adopt a child? Why or why not.

A Personal Invitation from the Author

If you have not made a decision to accept Jesus Christ as your personal Lord and Savior, God himself extends this invitation to you.

If you have not trusted Him and believed Him to be the giver of eternal life, you can do so right now. We do not know the second, the minute, the hour, the moment, or day that God will come to claim us. Will you be ready?

The Word of God says:

"If you confess with your mouth, 'Jesus is Lord,' and believe in your heart that God raised him from the dead, you will be saved. For it is with your heart that you believe and are justified, and it is with your mouth that you confess and are SAVED" (Romans 10:9-10 NIV, emphasis added).

To arrange signings, book events, or speaking engagements with the author,
contact books@shelialipsey.com

To send your personal comments to the author please contact:
Email: books@shelialipsey.com

Connect Via Social Media
http://twitter.com/shelialipsey
Shelia E. Lipsey Readers on Facebook
Urban Christian Authors Group on Facebook
Web site –www.shelialipsey.com
www.perfectstoriesaboutimperfectpeople.com
www.UCHisglorybookclub.net

Thank you for supporting my literary career!

Remember to

Live Your Dreams Now!

Shelia E. Lipsey, God's Amazing Girl

Book Order Form
Bonita And Hodge Publishing Group, LLC
P. O. Box 280202
Memphis, TN 38168

Name

Address ______________________________

City/State/Zip ______________________________

Quantity	Title(s)	Cost ea.	Total
	My Sister, My Momma, My Wife	10.00	
	My Son's Wife	10.00	
	My Son's Ex-Wife The Aftermath	10.00	
	My Son's Next Wife	10.00	
	Beautiful Ugly	10.00	
	True Beauty	10.00	
	Sinsatiable	10.00	
	Into Each Life	10.00	
	A Christian's Perspective - Journey Through Grief	7.00	
	Grand Total		

Shipping & Handling – add $3.50 for 1st book then $1.75 for each additional book.
Please send a Money order or cashiers' check payable to
Bonita And Hodge Publishing Group, LLC

CPSIA information can be obtained at www.ICGtesting.com
Printed in the USA
LVOW11s2123270315

432395LV00001B/20/P

9 780983 893523